# Chasing You

**Felicity Snow**

# Prologue

It was Cash's eyes that Emmett noticed first, as green as emeralds and brimming with curiosity, humor, and kindness. He was tall and slender with dark hair that stuck up in all directions, dressed in distressed black skinny jeans and a gray T-shirt, and wearing a corded bracelet around his left wrist. His voice was rich and deep, and when Cash smiled it almost took Emmett's breath away.

It was a Tuesday afternoon when he saw Cash out in the school parking lot helping a faculty member change a tire on their car. Even though it made his designer clothes filthy, the young man took it in stride, a warm smile on his face as he wiped his hands on his jeans and sweat from his forehead.

It was a Friday when Emmett saw him in the library after school, tutoring another student. He wasn't surprised to see how relaxed they both were. Cash just seemed to have a way with people. Most students would be nervous but Cash was charming, charismatic, and kind. He would make anyone feel like they could accomplish the task in front of them.

It was on Sunday mornings—when he worked side by

side with Cash at the homeless shelter and got to see the way his face lit up as the men, women, and families with small children came through the line for food—that he found himself drawn to the young man even more. He got to hear his infectious laughter as Cash went from table to table conversing with the members of the community, visiting with them as they ate.

He grew to cherish those moments when he was with Cash outside of the school walls, seeing him in another element, talking to him about how much he loved history and learning about other cultures; about how much Cash loved to travel and how he'd done service projects in several different countries on his summer vacations. It was on those Sunday mornings that Emmett heard about Cash's love of nature and how he rose early every morning before school because he loved watching the sun rise as his feet pounded the pavement and his music beat a steady rhythm in his ears, his muscles burning and his heart racing.

"It's sort of my outlet, you know?" Cash said one day as they were cleaning things up after the morning rush and wiping off tables. He had a slight flush on his cheeks and Emmett thought he must be embarrassed about how animatedly he'd talked about his runs, but he couldn't for the life of him figure out why. It was obviously something he was passionate about and that made Emmett smile.

"I do." Emmett nodded. "I don't get running in general," he added. "I'd rather have my intestines removed, but music is definitely an outlet for me."

Cash laughed. "Running's not your thing, huh?"

"Nah, I'm more of a couch potato. I work out because I have to, but I hate it. And I don't run unless someone is chasing me."

That got another chuckle out of Cash and he shook his head as he continued to wipe down the tables.

"So why the homeless shelter, and the service projects?" Emmett asked a moment later.

Cash shrugged. "Most people assume I'm doing it because it will look good on my college applications, but honestly, I just want to help. I see a need and I want to fill it. I think that's why we're here. To make life better for others. I know it's technically us helping them but actually I think it's the other way around. It does something for me that I can't really explain. It makes me happy. But I guess, if I'm being honest, it helps keep my mind off my own problems too, you know? And focused on the bigger picture."

Emmett hated the idea of Cash having problems or needing an outlet for anything, but of course he would have stresses in his life just like anyone else. High school wasn't easy, especially senior year, and he had no idea what Cash's home life was like. He hoped it was a positive environment. His own teenage years had been filled with strife: his parents' constant bickering, his own feelings of inadequacy and self-loathing over his sexuality, the guilt over tearing his family apart, the loneliness he'd felt when he'd lost friends because of his choice to be honest about who he was. Thankfully he'd had his sister or he didn't know what he would have done. And he'd had his music. He hadn't been kidding when he'd said it was an outlet for him. It always had been. It encouraged him, calmed him, relieved some of his anxiety, and reminded him that he wasn't alone.

"Well, if there's ever anything bothering you or you need someone to talk to, I'm always here. I hope you know that," he said.

Cash paused, looking up at Emmett through his long dark eyelashes. His green eyes studied Emmett intently before he said, "Thank you. I appreciate that." He gave Emmett a small smile.

As the weeks went on and Emmett saw more and more

of Cash, he found himself falling for him harder and harder. And it frightened him.

Because Emmett couldn't tell Cash how he felt. Emmett couldn't tell anyone. Hell, he'd been trying for a long time not to even tell himself.

Because Emmett was twenty-six years old, and Emmett was Cash's teacher.

The fact that he was interested in one of his students was, he knew, not okay.

At least, doing anything about it was not okay.

The feelings he couldn't help. He had tried. God had he tried. For months now he'd tried to ignore them, block them out, pretend they didn't exist, but it was no use.

Still he was determined to make it through the year without making an idiot out of himself or losing his job over the young man. That would be the worst possible mistake. He was a professional and he would handle this like one.

No one knew. No one was ever going to know.

Shame and guilt had been his new best friends in the past few months, ever since he'd developed these feelings for the dark-haired boy, and he was starting to think they weren't going to be fading any time soon.

On the plus side, winter break would be coming soon and he'd be getting a much-needed reprieve, and then just five short months after that the school year would be over, Cash would be graduating along with all the other seniors, and Emmett would never see him again.

That was what he wanted, right? To never see Cash again? To be rid of him, rid of these unwanted feelings.

Right?

———

"Mr. Jones?"

4

Emmett looked up from his desk to see Cash standing in his doorway. The young man was dressed in distressed dark wash jeans along with a form-fitting black T-shirt and Converse sneakers.

Emmett swallowed. He put his pen down, slid his reading glasses off his face, then cleared his throat.

"Hello, Cash. Can I help you?" He was already internally chastising himself for his attraction to the young man but kept his face stoic as Cash approached his desk. His dark hair had gotten longer and was sticking out in all directions, which Emmett told himself was not at all sexy and that Cash's eyes were not beautiful, and his heart was not beating faster as the young man sat in the chair opposite him.

"I, uh, I was wondering if you could do me a favor, actually," Cash said. "I'm working on applying for colleges, and I was hoping you could write me a letter of recommendation?" He said it as a question rather than a statement, his teeth tugging on his bottom lip as he gazed at Emmett, his eyes hopeful.

God that lip biting thing drove Emmett crazy. To his horror he felt his dick twitching, and he shifted in his seat, so incredibly thankful he was hidden by his desk. He flushed and was hopeful that somehow Cash didn't notice. A letter of recommendation? How the hell was he supposed to do that? Not that he couldn't find a million and one good things to write about the young man but he just felt like any letter of recommendation from him would be a tad biased. Still, he felt like he owed it to Cash to be a damn professional about this. What was he going to tell the kid? *No, sorry, I can't 'cause I think I'm in love with you? Yeah, no.* "Sure," he said. "I'd be happy to."

Cash beamed. "Thanks, Mr. Jones. I really appreciate it."

Cash had reached the doorway when he turned and said, "See you Sunday?"

Emmett smiled. "Of course. Wouldn't miss it." He let out a deep breath when Cash disappeared through the door.

*Graduation,* he told himself. *Just six more months til graduation and he'll be out of your life forever. You can do it, Emmett Jones.*


## Four months later

"Jesus," Emmett said, resting his hand on his chest and gasping.

Cash chuckled slightly. "Sorry. I didn't mean to scare you, Mr. Jones."

Emmett set his eraser down and examined his now empty whiteboard, then rubbed his hands together. "Don't sneak up on me like that," he said. "This job doesn't pay well enough for me to end up in the emergency room." His lips turned up at the corners in a small smile. Cash grinned and shook his head in bemusement. The classroom was empty save for the two of them, but the halls outside were bustling and the noise of students and teachers talking and scurrying by carried through the open door.

"What can I do for you?" Emmett asked, leaning against the side of his desk, his arms crossed over his chest. "Problem with the homework?" He was surprised when Cash blushed, a wide smile covering his handsome face.

"No, nothing like that," he replied. "I just thought I'd let you know that that letter of recommendation you wrote for me got me accepted into Stanford. And I got a scholarship." He gripped the straps of his backpack, his smile growing even wider.

Emmett grinned. It took everything in him not to pull Cash into his arms and give him a hug. "Really?" he said.

"You're sure it had nothing to do with your grades, or SAT scores, or any essays you wrote, or extracurricular activities?"

Cash blushed again, his gaze darting to the floor. The smile never left his face. "It may have had something to do with those," he said, "but I know your letter helped, so thank you. Stanford has been a dream of mine. I'm really excited." His eyes met Emmett's when he looked up.

*Fuck, he's beautiful.* "Well, I'm glad I could help, Cash." Emmett straightened his spine and cleared his throat. "You deserve it. You've worked very hard, and I know you've got a bright future. Just keep chasing your dreams, okay?"

"I will," Cash said. "Thank you again."

Emmett nodded and Cash walked away, giving him a small wave before he disappeared.

Fuck.

Four months had gone by and nothing had changed. And he hated it. Hated that every time he was in the young man's company his palms got sweaty and his heart beat faster. Hated that Cash's smile still made him weak in the knees and that looking into his eyes made his brain short-circuit.

Nobody had ever had this effect on him before.

Why was it that the first time he had strong feelings for someone, it had to be someone he couldn't have?

### Two months later

"What's the matter?" Emmett asked as Cash collapsed in the seat next to him. The energy and liveliness that the young man normally exuded were gone. In their place was a look of weariness and exhaustion. His shoulders sagged, his hair was even more tousled than usual, and sweat beaded on his forehead. "Worn out?"

"In a way," Cash said, wiping his hand across his forehead. He leaned over, resting his elbows on his legs and staring at the ground.

Emmett was never thrilled when he got roped into being one of the chaperones for the school dances. Honestly, he loved his job for the most part and the kids were great, but he also liked going home and being done when the school day was over, relaxing in front of his television with his beer and pretzels, wearing his pajamas and bathrobe, and not having to be bombarded with balloons and streamers or Taylor Swift blasting from the speakers. But while the hundreds of other juniors and seniors were out there dancing and mingling, Cash was looking like he was about to have a panic attack.

"Where's your date?" Emmett asked, not really sure what else to say. "Isn't she gonna miss you?"

Cash sighed as his leg bounced up and down. He ran his fingers through his hair. "I don't think so. She didn't seem to be enjoying herself much anyway."

"Oh," Emmett said. "Sorry to hear that."

"It's okay," Cash said. "It's my own fault. I never should have asked her. It wasn't fair. I kind of ruined her prom, I guess, which I feel bad about. But I couldn't ask who I..." He glanced over at Emmett, then trailed off, biting his lip and wringing his hands together.

God damn, that lip biting thing drove Emmett crazy every time. He wanted to reach over and pull that full bottom lip away from those teeth. Save it from the onslaught it was getting. But instead he said, "I'm sure it's not as bad as all that."

Cash shrugged and turned to face him. He took a deep breath and let it out. "If you went to prom with someone who swung the other way, and you didn't know it, wouldn't it kind of ruin things for you?"

Emmett blinked. "Oh. I, uh...I see." Shit, he really wished he could have thought of something more encouraging to say to the young man but he was tongue tied. Cash was gay? Shit, the boy he was so crazy about was actually interested in guys?

It didn't matter, though. Cash was graduating in a few weeks and then he would be off to Stanford, on the other side of the country, and Emmett would never see him again. Besides that, Cash was way too young for him. It would never work. And more than that, he would probably be horrified at the idea of dating one of his former teachers.

"I've been faking interest in dancing with her all night," Cash continued. "And I haven't kissed her, and I have no desire to, and it's exhausting, pretending to be something I'm not. I had to remind myself to tell her she looked pretty only because I knew it was the polite thing to do. God, I'm such a jerk." He buried his face in his hands. "She deserved better than this."

"Why did you ask her?" Emmett asked.

"Because I knew she wanted me to," Cash said with a sigh. "And I didn't have anyone else to ask."

Emmett nodded. "No one else you wanted to ask, or no one else you felt comfortable asking?"

Cash rubbed his neck with his hand. "More, uh... more the second one, I guess," he admitted.

"You know, being gay isn't anything to be ashamed of," Emmett found himself saying. "I'm sorry your prom wasn't everything you wished it could be either. Your date might be understanding, she might not be, I don't know. But remember what I said about chasing your dreams? That doesn't just apply to your career, Cash. If you aren't ready to be open about your sexuality I understand, but there's freedom in accepting who you are, and loving yourself for who you are. Trust me. Your dreams can involve love and romance too. With a boy. You don't have to settle. Or pretend."

Cash gave him a small smile, but Emmett noticed that it was a sad one. "Thank you, Mr. Jones," he said. He paused for a moment before speaking again, a slight quiver to his voice. "You, uh, you seem to know a lot about this. Are you...?" He gazed at Emmett, biting his lip again, his green eyes intense and questioning.

Emmett blushed, but smiled. "I'm bisexual."

Cash nodded. "And you're out?"

"As out as one can be, I think. My family knows. My friends know. I'm not saying it's all been sunshine and roses, but along the way I realized it was harder to hide my true self than it was to be honest, especially anytime I found myself interested in a guy. And the person I was really hurting in the end, was me, and it wasn't worth it. If I told people and they couldn't accept it, that was on them. And yeah, it hurt, when the friends or family I thought or hoped would stand by me didn't, but ultimately it was okay in the end because I was my authentic self, and that made me happier than my relationships with them.

"You'll find your tribe, Cash, and it might not be the people you thought it would be. And there will be a grieving period if you lose people, but there are people out there who will love you and support you, too, and you will also find tremendous freedom in living your own life as your truest self with someone that you love."

Cash nodded again. "Well, you've certainly given me some things to think about. Scares the shit out of me, but..."

Emmett chuckled. He was going to miss this kid.

He couldn't help but look Cash over briefly in his tux when the boy looked away. He was looking especially cute. He had a green bow tie on that matched his date's dress and happened to make his eyes stand out even more than usual, and his messy hair was absolute perfection.

More than anything he wished he could take Cash into his arms and lead him onto the dance floor, but that would be a big fat no no, so here they sat, teacher and student, talking to each other on prom night.

And Emmett found that he didn't want graduation to come so quickly anymore.

But graduation did come of course, and Emmett was thrilled when Cash took the stage to receive his diploma. He couldn't wipe the smile from his face as he applauded.

He was more than a little surprised when Cash approached him afterwards with his parents in tow and shook his hand.

"Thank you, Mr. Jones," he said. "For everything."

"My pleasure," Emmett said. He couldn't help but ask, "By the way, what are you studying in college, Cash?"

Cash grinned. "Education," he said. "Someone inspired me."

Emmett blushed. "Oh, I see," was all he could think to say. "Well, uh, I'm sure you'll do great."

"You've made a real impact on our son's life," Cash's mother said, shaking Emmett's hand. "He never stopped talking about you or your class."

Emmett blushed again. "He was an excellent student," he said. He looked into those beautiful emerald eyes one last time before the Christian family turned and walked away, and he knew that he would never see Cash again.

And something inside began to hurt.

# Chapter One

**Five years later**

E mmett groaned as the alarm on his phone went off and he reached over, fumbling around in the dark to grab it and turn it off. He tapped at it. He wasn't sure if he hit the snooze button or the off button, but it stopped and that was good enough for him.

He rubbed his eyes with the palms of his hands and yawned. For the love of all that was holy, why did he have to wake up at the butt crack of dawn? He was *not* a morning person and after three months of sleeping in, the cruel world was reminding him of it. He did this to himself every year, kept telling himself he'd adjust slowly to having to get up early again once the school year started but inevitably he failed. He just couldn't bring himself to go to bed early or wake up early if he didn't have to, so of course now he was paying for it.

But the warm arm around his chest and the soft lips pressed against his neck made the early morning hours a little more bearable, and he smiled despite his fatigue as he turned to face his fiancée.

"Morning, handsome," she said. She smiled softly at him as he tucked a strand of golden blonde hair behind her ear.

"Morning, beautiful," he replied, planting a kiss on her forehead.

"Summer break is over," she said, and stroked his cheek. "Ready for a new school year?"

Emmett hummed. "Ready as ever." He stroked her bare arm in return. She wore a light blue nightgown with spaghetti straps that he'd bought her for her birthday a few months back. She'd teased him at first, asking if it was really a gift for her or for him. He'd blushed and asked why it couldn't be both. But then she'd raved about how soft and comfortable it was and wore it frequently, and Emmett never tired of seeing her in it, not just because of the lace at the top, the cute bow in the center, and the way it hugged her curves in all the right places, but because she truly lit up every time she put it on.

He placed another kiss on her forehead, this one longer, and held her close. "I love you," he said, looking into her brown eyes once he'd pulled away.

"I love you, too," she said. She looked down at the ring on her finger and beamed, holding her hand up, and Emmett smiled back, taking her hand into his and kissing it gently. He pressed a soft kiss to her nose and then her lips before they climbed out of bed to get ready for work.

————

Forty-five minutes later, Emmett climbed out of his car dressed in a white dress shirt with his sleeves rolled up, exposing his forearms, a blue-and-white striped tie, and black slacks. His blond hair fell over his forehead and the blue in his tie made his sapphire eyes pop. He held a large cup of coffee in one hand with his messenger bag slung over his shoulder as he walked up the steps to the high school for the first day of classes.

He made it to his classroom, set his bag on the floor next to his chair, and sipped at his coffee. Taking a deep breath, he surveyed the room. Twenty-six chairs would soon be filled.

This was his seventh year teaching history at Anderson High School. He had a secure job that he loved and a wonderful home with a beautiful woman. He was getting married. Everything was just perfect.

It was going to be a good year.

———

After work, Emmett headed to his favorite coffee shop just around the corner from the school. Being at home would be boring and lonely without Harper there. She never got off work until six and the two hours he spent by himself waiting for her were torture sometimes, so he preferred to grade his papers and work on his lesson plans over a cup of joe at *Cozy Coffee* instead.

As he opened the door, the familiar sounds of low conversation, soft music, and the *tink-tink* of dishes greeted him, and he smiled. He'd gone here every day for the last several years and loved the atmosphere. They decorated for every holiday and season. Oftentimes he would run into his students working on their homework at the end of the day, and a few of them even had part-time jobs here after school. He'd find his favorite seat in the corner by the window, a large plush orange chair, and would wave occasionally as he spied people he knew through the window.

With it being fall, the coffee shop was decorated with multi-colored leaves and pumpkins on the tables and scattered across the counter, and the fresh scents of pumpkin spice and cinnamon filled the air. Emmett drank it in. He loved fall and everything that came with it, so he got in line to order his favorite pumpkin spice latte.

That was when he got a glimpse of something, or rather, someone in the corner of the cafe that made his heart stop, and he stared.

*Holy shit. Cash?* he thought. *That can't be Cash.* It had been five years since he'd seen the boy, but holy fuck, Cash wasn't a boy anymore. He'd grown up, and if possible he was even more handsome than when he'd been in high school. The same tousled dark hair of course, and striking green eyes, even from a distance, but his face was now covered in stubble and he was more filled out. More toned, less cute, Emmett thought, and more strikingly handsome. He wore dark wash jeans and a gray Henley under a green jacket.

*Fuck,* Emmett thought, *I should really stop staring. This is awkward. Oh God, he's looking up. He's looking at me. Jesus, what the fuck am I doing?*

Cash smiled at him and Emmett smiled back, feeling like an absolute ass. But now that Cash had spotted him he knew it would be rude not to go over and say hello, so after getting his latte he walked over to Cash's table, trying with every step not to show how terribly nervous he was. He gripped his latte in both hands to keep it and his hands from shaking.

"Mr. Jones, hi," Cash said, beaming. "Gosh, it's good to see you."

Emmett couldn't help but smile. "You, uh, you really don't have to call me Mr. Jones anymore, Cash," he said. "I'm not your teacher. Haven't been for a while."

Cash blushed. "Right, yeah, habit, I guess. Would you

16

like to sit?" He gestured to the chair Emmett was standing next to.

Emmett hesitated slightly but really couldn't think of a reason not to. "Sure," he said. Wouldn't hurt to catch up with one of his old students, right?

"So, how are you?" he asked, taking a sip of his latte.

"I'm good," Cash said. "Really good, actually."

"Oh?" God, he could stare into those eyes for an eternity. Shit, what was he thinking? He was engaged. He shifted in his seat and swallowed. "Stanford treated you well?" he asked.

"Stanford was amazing," Cash said with a wide grin. "Not gonna lie, I had my share of sleepless nights and panic attacks over last-minute papers and whatnot, but overall, I loved it. Just graduated last year."

"And you moved back home? To be close to family, I take it?"

"I, uh... yeah, partly," Cash said, and Emmett noticed he was blushing and doing that lip biting thing again.

Oh God. It had been five years. How was that still having an effect on him? No boner, thank God, but butterflies? Yes. In droves. He'd thought only teenagers had those. For fuck's sake, he was swooning. And then he realized what Cash had said.

He cocked his head and narrowed his eyes. "What's the other part?"

"Personal reasons, I guess," Cash said, looking down and running his finger along the rim of his cup.

Emmett nodded. "Those dreams we talked about," he said. "You chase them?"

Cash grinned. "Some. Working on others still."

Emmett smiled. "Good for you."

"I uh, I wanted to thank you, actually," Cash said. "For that talk on prom night my senior year. It really helped me, more than you'd realize. I told my parents about a year after I graduated high school."

"How'd they take it?"

Cash smiled. "They cried, actually," he said, and he noticed the confusion on Emmett's face and laughed slightly. "They said they had known I was gay for years but they were waiting for me to feel comfortable enough to tell them, and they were just happy that I finally felt safe enough to do it. They've been incredibly loving and supportive. I've been very lucky."

Emmett smiled. "I'm happy for you, Cash."

"Thanks, Mr., uh, I mean...Emmett," he stuttered and blushed slightly. "God, it feels weird calling you that."

Emmett was not going to tell Cash that it felt amazing hearing him say it, so he just smiled.

They continued to talk. Cash told Emmett about the overseas trips he'd made to Haiti and Guatemala while in college, building orphanages, playing soccer with the local kids, and on one very unfortunate occasion, getting a very bad case of food poisoning that had him praying for death for almost twenty-four hours.

Emmett never did get his lesson plans done, or even started, and he only looked at his phone and realized what time it was when it buzzed in his pocket and he saw that he had a text message from Harper.

"Oh shit," he said. "It's my fiancée. I gotta go."

"You're engaged?" Cash said, and Emmett swore he saw the light leaving Cash's eyes and heard genuine despair in his voice, but he told himself his brain was just playing tricks on him.

"Yeah, her name's Harper. Been together for a couple of years now," he said with a smile. "Planning a December wedding. She wants there to be a winter theme. She's got this thing for snowflakes and freezing your ass off." He grinned, and Cash tried to return it but it was a sad attempt.

"It was nice seeing you again, Cash," Emmett said, standing and grabbing his messenger bag. "Maybe I'll see you around if you frequent this place."

"Yeah." Cash stood. "It was good seeing you too, Emmett. Congratulations on the engagement."

"Thanks," Emmett said, smiling. He waved and walked away, but if he'd turned around he would have noticed the tear that slid ever so silently down Cash's cheek.

# Chapter Two

Cash couldn't remember the last time he'd pushed his body this hard. His side was aching, his legs throbbed and his lungs burned. He had sweat dripping down his back and falling into his eyes as he ran. He wasn't sure at this point how many miles it had been. Six? Seven? But he couldn't stop. *The Greatest Showman* soundtrack played through his earbuds as his feet pounded the pavement over and over again, as he made his way through the familiar path of the park he'd frequented as a teenager.

It wasn't long before he had to force himself to stop and lean against a tree, panting and feeling the ache in his side so acutely it made him grimace. The ache in his heart was ten times worse, though, and the sweat dripping down his forehead began to mingle with the tears sliding down his cheeks as he slid to the ground, sobbing quietly.

It had been ages since he'd cried. Maybe he was naive and foolish to have even thought that after all these years Mr. Jones—Emmett—might have still been available, and that if he were available he'd have any interest in dating a former student, but Cash had had a hopeless crush on the man since his senior year. It had scared the ever-loving shit out of him when he'd realized it. When he'd realized that Mr. Jones was the one he wanted to ask to prom and no one else would do. When he'd imagined what it would be like to kiss him and hold his hand. When he'd realized that the man's smile made his heart flutter. He had a passion for teaching and learning that Cash had found infectious and a love for his students that was nothing but endearing. He'd been more than a teacher to Cash. He'd been a mentor and a friend, and Cash had hoped, dreamed, that maybe after graduation, after college, they could be something more.

## Five years earlier

"You okay, sweetheart?" Cash's mom asked as the minivan drove down the street past the gas station and the local Walmart. Past the nail salon, the florist, and the local preschool, on their way to the interstate, where they would be making the long drive to California and Stanford. The AC was blasting to try and beat the August heat and the radio played softly.

Cash gazed out the window and sighed, feeling an ache in his chest as they reached the high school and kept right on driving. It felt like he was leaving something utterly precious behind. "Yeah," he said. But he couldn't help thinking of a certain blond-haired teacher with freckles and blue eyes, remembering their conversations on Sunday mornings at the homeless shelter, the night of his prom when Mr. Jones had sat with him and talked, the way his smile made Cash's heart beat faster, how his kindness and compassion touched something in him that he couldn't explain. As much as he wanted to chase his dreams at Stanford he hated the idea of leaving and not knowing what would happen to his former teacher. Would he start dating someone? Would he get married? The thought made Cash sick to his stomach and he knew he cared for him more than he probably should, but he couldn't help it. He was drawn to him, had been for months now. And one of two things was going to happen—he would forget all about Mr. Jones at Stanford, or he would come back home and do whatever it took to get the older man to realize that the two of them belonged together.

"Thought you would be more excited," his dad commented from the driver's seat, pulling Cash out of his thoughts. "Stanford and California. You've been really looking forward to this." He looked at Cash through the rearview mirror, studying him.

"No, yeah, I am," Cash stammered. "Just a little nervous, too, I guess." He gave his dad a small smile and his parents exchanged glances, but Cash just shrugged it off and turned back to looking out the window.

*Stanford here I come.* He took in a deep breath and let it out, running his fingers through his dark hair. *Mr. Jones, please wait for me. I know I'm eighteen and you're twenty-six but I swear we're meant to be together. I think I'm already in love with you.*

## Present day

But Cash had been wrong. It was too late now. Emmett was engaged. He was getting married in three months, and he had no idea that when he had told Cash to chase his dreams all those years ago, Cash's biggest dream had been him.

He had no idea that Cash had come back to Anderson hoping to run into him, to eventually screw up the courage to ask him out, to see what would happen. He had no idea that every other guy Cash had dated had only lasted a few weeks because in his heart he knew they weren't for him, because they weren't his former teacher. Despite their age difference, and their history, Cash just couldn't picture himself with anyone else.

But some dreams, it seemed, just weren't meant to be.

So he sat there, arms covering his face, tears sliding down his cheeks. When he wiped them away, more followed.

And he found himself being very jealous of one Miss Harper Soon-To-Be-Jones.

———

"Hey, earth to Emmett." Emmett felt a tap on his knee and turned to face his fiancée.

"Hmm?" he asked.

Harper sighed and pulled his hand away from his mouth where his middle finger had been wedged between his teeth. "Keep that up and you won't have any nail left," she said, frowning.

Emmett looked down at the nail he'd been biting and grimaced. He hadn't even realized he'd been doing it.

"Hey, what's up with you?" Harper asked, not unkindly. "Are you okay?"

"Yeah, of course," Emmett said. In all fairness though, he had been distracted lately. It had been a few days since he'd seen Cash at *Cozy Coffee* and he hadn't been able to get the other man out of his mind. It scared him, how attracted he still was to him, how much he'd enjoyed seeing him again, being with him, talking to him as an adult and realizing that all the things that had attracted him to Cash as a teenager were still just as attractive now. His compassion and tenderness, his vivacious spirit, his kindness, his beauty. And it was thoughts like that which had him sitting on the couch trying to grade papers and staring into the distance biting his nail off instead, feeling guilty as hell.

"Em, I called your name three times and you didn't hear me," Harper said from her place on the floor in front of the coffee table. She had a trace of worry in her voice. "Your head has been in the clouds lately. What's going on?" She kept his hand in hers and stroked it with her thumb. "You know you can talk to me, right?"

Emmett gave her a gentle smile. He reached over and stroked her cheek. "I know," he said softly.

"Is it work?" she asked, prodding.

"It's nothing, babe," he said and pressed his lips to her fingers. Whether he was trying to reassure himself or her, he wasn't sure. "Don't worry. I'm here. What is it?"

"Emmett Jones, I've known you long enough to know that when you bite your middle finger, it's not nothing," she stated. "What's bothering you? You were super quiet during dinner. You hardly ate anything, and you've been distant the past few days."

Emmett sighed. "I'm sorry I've been a crappy fiancé," he said, moving his papers aside and joining her on the floor. "It's nothing you need to worry about. I promise. It'll work itself out. I'm probably overthinking it myself." He took her face into his hands and kissed her tenderly, reminding himself how much he loved her and how good it felt to hold her, touch her. "Now, what is it?" he asked, pulling away and looking into her warm brown eyes.

She gave him a soft smile. "I wanted to ask your opinion on place settings for the wedding. What do you think? Rectangular name cards or snowflakes to go with our theme?"

"Snowflakes, all the way," he replied, giving her a warm smile.

Harper beamed. "I agree." She kissed him. "Our reception is going to be so beautiful, Em." She sighed and rested her head on his shoulder.

"Of course it will be. You'll be there." He nudged her slightly and she blushed and shook her head at him fondly.

"You're ridiculously corny and incredibly sweet," she replied, then kissed him again. "That's why I love you." There was a pause before she spoke again, a look of uncertainty in her eyes.

"Are you sure you don't want to invite your dad?" she asked.

Emmett's body tensed immediately at the mention of his father, and he felt a familiar tightness in his chest. "Positive," he said.

"You sure he wouldn't want to come?" Harper asked. "We have room." She gestured to the mock seating arrangements laid out across the coffee table.

"It doesn't matter. I don't want him there." Emmett's voice was firm leaving no room for argument.

Harper nodded. "Okay," she said and kissed his cheek. "Help me figure out the rest of these place settings?"

Emmett nodded.

They spent the next hour working on wedding stuff, and then Emmett finally did get some grading done before they crawled into bed together. Harper nestled against his chest and he slid his arm around her as they fell asleep.

# Chapter Three

"Hey, handsome," Cash heard from his left and turned to see a tall gorgeous man next to him smiling flirtatiously. His slender body moved fluidly as he stepped closer and slid his finger along Cash's arm. He had more makeup on than Cash was accustomed to, glitter eyeshadow and shiny pink lip gloss, but he had to admit it made his light blue eyes stand out and his handsome features shine. He was pretty sure there was even glitter in his spiked blond hair. "You here alone, cutie?" he asked, a slight lisp to his voice that Cash found adorable.

"Uh." Cash cleared his throat. "Yeah, I guess." He didn't stop the man from touching him, his fingers moving across his shoulder and the back of his neck.

"You guess?" the man said and laughed slightly, giving him a smile. "Don't you know?"

Cash couldn't help but smile back. He looked the man over in his tight-fitting pink T-shirt and snug white jeans. He really was gorgeous. Even so, Cash didn't feel himself reacting at all, not even when the man leaned in and whispered, "Wanna get out of here?"

Still, he found himself grabbing his jacket and nodding.

He didn't know what it was going to take for him to get over Emmett Jones but maybe this was a start.

———

"So this is it," the man said as he led Cash into his apartment. It was simple, the living room as soon as you entered, the kitchen beyond that. To the left was a hallway, which he assumed led to the bathroom and the bedroom. Beige carpet covered the floor and there were a few small plants scattered about, along with some photos of family and friends. Modern artwork covered the walls.

"It's nice," Cash said as he looked around, shoving his hands in his pockets. God, was he really doing this? Hookups weren't his thing. He'd never had sex with a random stranger before, but he was so beside himself he just didn't know what to do. Maybe fucking someone else would get Emmett off his mind, at least for a little while. Still, he wasn't at all horny.

Even when Gorgeous stepped forward and began unbuttoning Cash's coat, their faces only inches apart, Cash didn't feel a thing. Even when his coat fell to the floor along with the other man's, nothing stirred inside him.

"You want to know my name?" Gorgeous asked as he leaned forward and planted kisses on Cash's neck, unbuttoning his shirt as he did so. Cash lifted his head to grant him access, but he immediately started chastising himself when images of Emmett started filling his mind.

"Shit," he whispered.

"What?" Gorgeous asked, pulling away slightly and gazing at him.

Cash bit his lip. "Nothing," he said. "What's your name?" Maybe if he knew the man's name, it would be easier not to think of Emmett while they were fucking.

"Avery," he said, the *r* sounding like a *w*, his voice soft and sweet. He smiled as he finished with the buttons on Cash's shirt and slid it off his shoulders and onto the floor. His gaze roamed over Cash's torso and he grinned even wider. "Damn, baby, you hot," he said as his eyes made their way back to Cash's, his hands sliding up his bare chest.

Cash flushed and swallowed as Avery pressed close to him, and he gasped when he felt the other man's hard cock pressed against his leg and Avery's lips on his neck once again. Avery must have mistaken his discomfort for pleasure because he purred and pressed in closer, licking and sucking on his ear.

*Try harder, you jackass.* Cash tilted his head and caught Avery's gloss-slicked lips with his, kissing him hungrily. He tasted like strawberries and peppermint. He tugged on the other man's T-shirt until Avery stepped back and let Cash pull it over his head, smiling. Then he was back, their chests pressed together, their bodies flush. Avery's hand gripped the back of his neck, the other his hip, and his erection pressed against Cash once again, grinding lasciviously. Although Cash was kissing him hard, their tongues dancing, their breathing heavy, his cock was as soft as ever.

"Hey," Avery said, pulling away. "What's wrong?" His blue eyes studied Cash with concern.

"No-nothing," Cash replied, and he tried to kiss Avery again. But Avery backed away, shaking his head.

"You're not into this," he said. "Are you?" He didn't sound angry, just resigned.

Cash opened his mouth to deny it but then closed it again. "I'm sorry," he said. He tugged at his hair in frustration. "I want to be. Truly I do. You're gorgeous, and you seem really nice."

To his surprise, Avery smiled. "Don't worry about it, babe," he said. "If it's not for you, it's not for you. I just hope you figure out whatever it is that's got you so in knots." He leaned over and picked Cash's shirt and coat up off the floor and handed them to him.

"Thanks," Cash said as he dressed himself. "Sorry to leave you hanging." He gestured to Avery's groin and Avery giggled.

"I've got ways of taking care of that, don't you worry," he said. "You take care of yourself, okay?"

Cash nodded, sliding on his coat. "Thank you," he said, his gazing flitting over the strange yet fascinating man he'd run into by accident. "I can honestly say I hope I see you again, Avery."

Avery smiled. "Me, too, uh..."

"Cash," Cash said, smiling.

Avery nodded. "Goodnight, Cash. I hope things work out between you and your man."

Cash's eyes widened. "How did you—"

"I'm as smart as I am beautiful," Avery said, his hand on his hip. He waved. "Goodnight, handsome."

"Goodnight," Cash said, opening the door and shutting it behind him.

He'd only made it a few steps when the tears started filling his eyes again, and before he knew it, he had pulled into the driveway of his parents' house and was ringing the doorbell.

"Hi, Mom," he said, tears sliding down his cheeks when she opened the door in her nightgown and bathrobe, her brown hair down around her shoulders.

"Cash," she said, taking him in her arms in an instant. "Sweetheart, what are you doing here? It's after midnight." Her voice was laced with concern as she rubbed his back.

Cash shook his head as he continued to sob and his mom brought him into the house, walking him over to the sofa and sitting next to him. He rested his head on her shoulder and cried softly.

"Nancy?" A gruff voice came from the stairs. "What's going on?"

"I don't know." She turned to look at her husband. "He hasn't told me."

Patrick Christian was an average-sized man with a large stomach and a nearly bald head that Cash continually prayed he wouldn't inherit, but as big as his belly was, his heart was just as big. His father adored his family, and that made him the best man in the world in Cash's eyes. He loved both of his parents more than anything. And more than anything, he needed them right now.

"Hey, slugger," Patrick said, sitting beside Cash on the sofa. "What's going on?"

Cash lifted his head and sniffled, wiping at his tears. "Hi, Dad."

"Hi," Patrick said, eyeing him. "Good to see you. Nice night for a visit. Why are you sobbing on your mother's shoulder like the dog just got run over?"

"Patrick," Nancy scolded, reaching over to slap him but hitting Cash instead.

"Ow, Mom, I'm a very innocent bystander," Cash said, jerking away.

"I'm sorry, sweetie." Nancy wrapped her arms around him and squeezed him to her chest. "Now tell us what's wrong."

Cash's chest heaved and he felt more tears brimming. "Shit. I'm such a fucking mess."

"We can see that, son," his dad said, and Nancy glared at her husband again. Patrick rolled his eyes. "What's his name?"

"Jesus Christ, Patrick, have you no decorum?" Nancy retorted.

"Well, we all know that's what it is," he said.

Nancy looked down at Cash, still clutching him tightly. "Is it?" He nodded, tears sliding down his cheeks again. As embarrassed as he was, he couldn't help it.

"Oh, honey, what happened?"

Cash's tears flowed freely now. "He's engaged." He sobbed, clutching his mother's arm and burying his face in her chest.

"Who's engaged?" Nancy asked, stroking her fingers through his hair.

"E...Emmett." He could barely get the man's name out through his sobs.

"You mean that teacher you've been in love with for the last five years?" his dad said.

"Oh, for Christ's sake, Patrick," Nancy chided. "Learn when to keep your mouth shut."

"Why? This is easier."

Cash's heart was beating out of his chest. "You knew?" he said, sitting up.

"Yes, sweetheart, you made it pretty obvious," Nancy said.

Cash flushed. "Oh. I didn't...I didn't realize. And you never said anything? Weren't you worried?"

"That you were gonna shack up with your teacher? No, of course not. You were both too smart for that. And you weren't even out at the time. There's no way you would let yourself get caught doing something like that. Besides, you were eighteen, and if you wanted to pursue something after you graduated, that was up to you," Patrick said.

"Well, it's too late now," Cash said, wiping away tears again. "He doesn't want me." His gaze dropped to the floor. "He never wanted me." He began to cry again.

"Oh, honey," Nancy said. "I'm so sorry."

"Why don't I go make us some tea?" Patrick stood and made his way into the kitchen.

"Honey, I know this is hard," Nancy said, rubbing his back. "I know. Maybe things will work out for you two in the end. You never know. Life has a way of surprising us."

"I don't think so, Mom," Cash said, wiping at his nose with the tissue she handed him. "I don't know how it could. I just need to figure out how to move on, and I don't know how."

"Oh. Well, maybe you just need time, sweetheart." She leaned down and kissed his head. She waited until Patrick had returned and Cash was sipping on his drink, his face drawn and his eyes red rimmed. "Why don't you sleep here tonight?" she suggested. "You can have your old room."

Cash really wanted to tell his mom that he was fine, that he didn't need to stay over. But he gave her a small smile and nodded because he did need that. He was hurting, and he needed to be taken care of.

He finished his tea and borrowed some of his dad's pajamas, and then crawled into his old bed. His room had been transformed into a guest room, and the movie posters and pictures of his friends and his school awards had been replaced with floral arrangements and paintings of gardens and small children. He smiled because it made him think of his mother. And in his old room, in his old house, he let his mother tuck him in and kiss his cheek before he finally dozed off.

# Chapter Four

E mmett moaned as Cash's tongue slid into his mouth. He was pressed up against the wall and Cash was kissing him hard, and Emmett was running his fingers through the young man's hair, kissing him back. His heart was racing. God, this was everything he'd ever wanted. Damn, Cash was a good kisser, and he felt amazing, and his hair was so soft, and thick, and his lips were perfection, and Cash's body was so warm and strong pressed against his, and...and then music.

Music?

What the hell?

They pulled apart and looked around.

"Emmett," he heard, and then felt a much softer, gentler hand on his arm. "Emmett, wake up," Harper said, nudging him. "The alarm is going off, baby."

Emmett's eyes opened and he was breathing heavily. He reached over to shut off the alarm and then ran his hand over his face, his heart racing. Holy shit. What the fuck was that? He'd never had any sort of even semi-erotic dream about Cash before, even with all of the feelings he'd had for the man in the past. And those feelings were in the past, right?

What the fuck?

It was just a dream, he told himself. But, shit, he had one hell of a hard-on.

"You okay, babe?" Harper asked as he ran his fingers through his hair.

"Huh?" he said, looking over at her now.

"You okay?" she asked again, scooting closer to him and resting her hand on his chest. He wrapped his arms around her and kissed her head.

"Yeah," he said, and he did find that having her in his arms made him feel better. "Yeah, I'm good."

It was just a dream.

———

Emmett rubbed at the sleep in his eyes and tried to stifle a yawn. It was all he could do to keep his eyes open as he clutched the world's largest cup of coffee in his hand, wondering what on earth they all had to be in at seven in the frickin' morning for on a Wednesday. On top of that, he was hating himself because for the past three weeks he'd had the same dream about a certain dark-haired man with emerald eyes that he just couldn't seem to shake. It was driving him insane and making him feel tremendously guilty at the same time. He hadn't been able to get Cash out of his mind no matter how hard he tried. He knew he couldn't control his dreams, and it wasn't like he was searching Cash out or having little trysts with him behind Harper's back or anything. But still, part of him couldn't help feeling bad about the fact that while she was busy planning their wedding and asking him about flowers and decorations, and music for the reception, he was having erotic dreams about a guy.

He still hadn't seen Cash since the coffee shop, and he'd been very intentional about being more present with Harper and not allowing himself to get distracted with thoughts of Cash. In fact, he'd intentionally avoided the coffee shop so that he wouldn't run into him, ever since the dreams had started, because God knew that would be all kinds of awkward, and he didn't want to do anything to jeopardize his relationship with Harper. Telling his fiancée that he was having sexual dreams about a former student that he'd truthfully once been very much into would be bad enough, but if she thought he was meeting up with him on occasion, it really wouldn't look good.

He wasn't about to throw what he had with Harper away, not for something that would never work in a thousand years anyway. Whatever feelings he'd had for Cash were in the past. The distant past. He'd moved on, and he was happy. Harper made him happy. Tying the knot would cement things for him, in his heart and mind, so the sooner this wedding happened, the better.

"Sorry for the early morning, everyone," Principal Newcomb said, addressing the room full of exhausted teachers and staff, "but we had a phone call from Mrs. White last night and she's informed us that she's been instructed by her doctor to be on bed rest until her baby is born. She'll be at home for the foreseeable future and we've hired a teacher to take her place. I wanted to introduce him to you. He should be here any minute. He's actually a former student who just graduated from Stanford and has taken this position very last minute, so he's doing us a big favor."

Emmett's eyes widened as Cash stepped into the doorway just then and knocked. He was suddenly very much awake. *Holy fucking shit. No, no, no, no, no. This cannot be happening. I can't work with him. Oh God, I think I might pass out.* He gripped the collar of his shirt and pulled on it and then swallowed.

"Am I on time?" Cash asked.

"Yes, Mr. Christian," Principal Newcomb said. "Please, come in."

Cash entered and stood next to the principal, his messenger bag slung over his shoulder. He wore slacks and a navy blue dress shirt, untucked, with a red tie, and Emmett found himself swallowing and thinking just how attractive Cash looked in his "teacher" attire and...fuck, he was *not* thinking of him like that anymore. Damn it. Damn that boy and his fucking gorgeousness.

"Mr. Christian will be taking over Mrs. White's history classes," Principal Newcomb said. "We're glad to have him on board and we hope that you will make him feel welcome. Emmett, would you be willing to show Mr. Christian to his classroom once we're finished here?" Principal Newcomb asked. "It's right next to yours."

"Of course," Emmett said, and gave Cash a smile, because he was, after all, a goddamn professional and he could pull himself together and work with his former student.

"Please, have a seat, Mr. Christian," Mr. Newcomb said, and they continued with their morning meeting for a few more minutes.

And Emmett just felt more and more guilty as the meeting went on because, try as he might, he couldn't keep his eyes off of Cash.

*Oh shit,* he thought, burying his head in his hands once the meeting was over and the other teachers were leaving. *I am so screwed.*

"You ready?" he heard, and looked up to see Cash waiting in front of him.

"Yeah, yeah, I'm..." Emmett stammered, grabbing his things and standing up.

"Honestly, I don't think I need the help. I remember this place pretty well," Cash said as they walked, "but since our classrooms are across the hall from each other and Mr. Newcomb asked you already, I figured we might as well..."

"Makes sense," Emmett agreed, but he didn't make eye contact. The combination of Cash's deep voice and the smell of his citrus cologne was enough to give him goose-bumps, and he found his heart beating faster in the young man's presence. *Shit, I have to get it together if I'm gonna be working with him for the next several months,* he told himself as they walked.

"You okay?" Cash asked. "You seem tired."

"Yeah," Emmett said, running his fingers through his hair and then lifting up his coffee cup and chuckling a little. "How could you tell?"

Cash chuckled too. "That's the zero-to-four hours size right there," he said. "I recognize that all too well from my college days. Coffee kept me alive half the time."

"Yeah," Emmett said.

"Work stress keeping you up?" Cash prodded gently. Emmett knew he wasn't trying to be nosy, just conversational and kind, but he obviously wasn't going to tell the young man the real reason for his lack of sleep. *Nah, truth is I've been dreaming about us having steamy make-out sessions for the past three weeks.* Nope. Time for a big-ass motherfucking lie.

"Mostly wedding stuff, I guess," he said. "I'm looking forward to it, of course, but it's stressful. Sometimes I wish we could just go to the courthouse and call it a day, not have to worry about all the hubbub. But it's important to Harper, and I get it. It's something to be celebrated. When it all comes down to it, I want it too. I just wish it were simpler."

Cash nodded. "Makes sense," he said. "I think I'd feel the same way."

"You, uh, you seeing anyone?" Emmett asked.

Cash shook his head. "There were a few guys in college but nothing that lasted."

"So, does that mean that you're out now? I mean, I know you told your parents, but..."

Cash smiled a little. "I mean, I'm not shouting it from the rooftops or anything, but yeah, I'm not hiding it either. And it feels pretty good, I gotta say. Being me."

Emmett beamed.

They were at Cash's classroom now, and he unlocked the door and stepped inside.

"First year teaching," Emmett said. "You gonna be okay with all these hormonal seventeen-year-olds?"

Cash smirked. "I think I'll manage," he said. "If I need any help, I know where to find you."

Emmett grinned. "I'm always here if you need me, Cash," he said. "Good luck."

———

"Hey, sweetheart, how did your first day of teaching go?"

"It was good, I think," Cash said to his mom over the phone as he heated up what was either an early dinner or a late lunch in the microwave. "I learned I have excellent bladder control and an endless amount of patience."

Nancy laughed. "Well, those will both come in handy if you ever have children."

Cash laughed too. "Yeah, I'm sure they will."

"It was okay, working with Emmett?" Nancy asked.

Cash sighed. "It was what it was. I made the best of it,

Mom. It's hard because I want to be around him, you know, but I can't be as close as I want to be, and I'm so afraid of messing up, doing something I shouldn't.'"

"You'll be okay," Nancy assured him. "I know this is hard for you, Cash, but it's only temporary. And sometimes difficult things have a way of turning out in our favor. You never know what will happen."

Cash smiled ruefully. "Okay, Mom. I gotta go and eat my dinner. Talk to you later, okay?"

"Okay, sweetheart. I love you. Bye."

"Bye, Mom."

———

"Hey, you," Harper said, smiling at Emmett as he reached her and gave her a kiss. "How was work?"

"Uh, good, yeah," he said, sweat gathering on the back of his neck and his palms. Why was he feeling guilty for having spent the day working with Cash when he'd had absolutely nothing to do with it? He hadn't hired him, and he hadn't followed him around or anything. Still, that intense desire to be in his presence felt overwhelming sometimes, and the guilt that was weighing on him for the insane attraction he felt toward the man was eating him alive. He'd had stomach pain for a good portion of the day, tension headaches that he was fairly certain were due to stress, and he'd had trouble focusing, and he was fairly certain it was all Cash's fault. He didn't know if he was more turned on or pissed off, and he wasn't sure if he wanted to punch the man or make out with him.

No, he was pretty sure which one of those he wanted to do, actually.

*No, stop.* Fuck. Oh fucking hell, he was meeting Harper to work on their wedding registry and he was fantasizing about Cash. Fuck, fuck, fuck. This was not happening. *Focus. Focus on Harper.*

"Em, you okay?" her soft voice asked, breaking through his turmoil.

"Yeah, just tired," he said. "Long day. I've got a bit of a headache."

"Oh, I'm sorry," she said sincerely. "Well, we can get a snack first at the Starbucks, then work on finishing up the registry. How does that sound?"

Emmett took her hand in his and squeezed it. Harper was one of the most thoughtful people he knew, which was what made her such a good nurse. He smiled as he remembered their first meeting. He'd had a sore throat for several days and had gone into the local urgent care clinic and come out with Harper's number. It had taken him a few days to get over his bout of strep throat, but once he had he'd called her up and they'd gone to dinner together, and the rest was history. She'd made him laugh and smile, and he'd enjoyed hearing about her work and how she put her heart into caring for others. She'd accepted right away that he was bisexual. It hadn't fazed her a bit. She'd truly admired the fact that he was a teacher. And it was remembering all of these things that made him breathe a little easier as they walked into Target hand in hand.

# Chapter Five

"Hey, this is exciting, huh?" Cash said as they boarded the plane for Washington, DC a month later. He was wearing jeans and a Stanford hoodie with his coat slung over his arm. His duffel bag rested over his other shoulder. "I remember doing this as a senior. Can't believe I'm a chaperone now."

Emmett, however, appeared far less excited. Cash had noticed from the moment they'd found their departure gate he'd been staring out the large window biting his middle finger, his leg bouncing up and down, and he seemed a little pale. He'd had his earbuds in and attached to his phone, so Cash hadn't bothered him, but he'd been curious about his behavior. He seemed to be radiating anxiety, and when Cash looked back at him as they made their way down the aisle, he saw that he had a death grip on his phone and his hand was shaking.

"This is us," Cash said, stopping in the aisle. He hefted his duffel into the overhead compartment and slid into the row of seats. Emmett followed, his phone and earbuds still clutched tightly in his hand. He breathed heavily as he took his seat next to Cash.

"Emmett, are you okay?" Cash asked finally, and only then did Emmett seem to realize that he was biting his nail and bouncing his leg up and down. His other hand gripped the armrest so tightly his knuckles were turning white, and they hadn't even left the ground yet.

Emmett released his grip on the armrest and stopped biting his finger, but he couldn't hide the fact that his hands were still shaking. He leaned forward and folded them together on his lap instead, then started running his fingers through his hair.

"I, uh, I don't fly very well," he admitted. "Kind of freaks me out, actually." He flushed and swallowed, a slight quiver to his voice.

"Oh," Cash said. "I didn't know that. Is there anything I can do to help?" He hated seeing Emmett so upset, his sapphire eyes filled with trepidation. It made him ache with the desire to protect the other man, to comfort him.

Emmett must have seen something in the way Cash looked at him, heard the genuine care in his voice, because he seemed to relax a little. "Distract me, maybe," he said and immediately flushed, seemingly embarrassed.

But Cash just gave him a small smile and nodded. "I'll do my best," he said. "Will it help if you have the window seat?"

Emmett shrugged. "I don't know. Maybe."

"Worth a try," Cash said. "Come on, let's switch."

"Any better?" Cash asked when Emmett was peering out the window.

"I think so," he replied. "Feeling slightly less claustrophobic and anxious. Thank you." He gave Cash a small smile and Cash smiled back.

The flight attendants came down the aisle for the inflight instructions. Emmett's breathing picked up again as the plane jostled and started moving down the runway, preparing for takeoff, and he gripped the armrests once again.

Cash looked over at his former teacher. He couldn't help but feel sorry for him. He'd had no idea the man was so afraid to fly, yet here he was doing it anyway for his students so that they could go on this trip to their nation's capital.

Washington, DC was supposed to be absolutely beautiful in the gorgeous late fall weather, and also considerably cheaper than in the spring, so the school was doing the trip in mid-November this year with some of the junior and senior class. Emmett and Cash had both been asked to chaperone. Cash had been thrilled for the opportunity, especially since he didn't have to pay for it. Emmett, clearly, not so much.

More than anything right now, Cash wished he could reach over and take the other man's hand into his, squeeze it gently, or stroke his thumb over Emmett's soft skin to soothe him, comfort him, ground him.

But he knew that if he did, it wouldn't be just about comforting Emmett. It would be about wanting to touch him, feel him, and he couldn't do that. He'd been trying for the past six weeks to get over Emmett Jones, to accept the fact that his former teacher was getting married and he was going to have to find another dream to chase. Even if it would probably be taken as a friendly, platonic gesture by everyone else around him, he couldn't take the other man's hand, even for a second. Because it would be a second too long.

"Hey, look at me," he said instead. And Emmett did, his sapphire eyes wide with fear. "I have an idea. This is gonna sound kinda corny but just go with me on it, okay?"

Emmett nodded. "I'm up for anything," he said. "Shoot."

"You know the movie *The Sound of Music*?"

"Yeah," Emmett said, sounding skeptical, his eyebrow raised. "You wanna watch a musical?"

Cash chuckled. "No. You remember the scene where there's a thunderstorm, and the kids are all running into Maria's room 'cause they're scared, and she sings that song about their favorite things to cheer them up?"

"You want to sing?" Emmett said, raising both eyebrows, his eyes getting even bigger.

Cash laughed again. "No. Will you stop?"

"Sorry," Emmett murmured, resting his head back against the seat and trying to just focus on taking one breath after another.

"But we are going to *talk* about our favorite things."

Emmett raised his eyebrow again, turning to look at Cash.

"We're gonna play a game of sorts," Cash said. "Taking turns listing our favorite things. And by the time we're done, the plane will be up in the sky and it will be smooth sailing, okay?"

"If you say so," Emmett said.

"I do."

"You go first. This was your idea."

"Okay. Ice cream," Cash stated with a grin.

"What kind?"

"Cookie dough."

"Rocky road," Emmett said, and he had a slight smile on his face now too.

"Chocolate lover or nut lover?" Cash asked.

"Both," Emmett said. "And don't forget the marshmallows."

"Ahh, right," Cash said.

"Ooh, that reminds me, s'mores." Emmett licked his lips and Cash laughed.

"Can't argue with that."

"And camping," Emmett said with a sigh and a starry-eyed look on his face as he rested his head back against the seat again. "And stargazing. And hot chocolate."

Cash smiled. "With marshmallows?"

Emmett turned his head and looked at him. "Of course," he said with a grin. There was a pause.

"Green," Emmett said, his eyes locked with Cash's.

"Huh?"

"My favorite color," Emmett said softly. "It's green."

"Blue," Cash replied without missing a beat.

Their gazes lingered on each other for a long moment before Cash said, "I didn't know you liked camping so much."

"Yeah," Emmett replied, clearing his throat and facing forward again. "We used to go all the time when I was a kid, as a family. My parents and my sister and me. It's been a while, though. I don't really have anyone to go with anymore."

"Why not?"

Emmett shrugged. "My sister's out in California. My parents got divorced when I was a freshman in college and Harper's not really a big fan. We went once but she was pretty miserable, so I haven't taken her again since."

"Sorry to hear that," Cash said. "I don't think I've ever been."

Emmett stared at him, dumbstruck. "Seriously?"

Cash shrugged. "My parents were never big on nature. Family vacations for us were always a bit more upscale. The Hilton, for instance. Swimming pools, resorts, that kind of thing."

"Well, you should try it sometime," Emmett said.

"Maybe I should," Cash agreed. "Have to find someone to go with me, though."

There was a moment of silence before Emmett spoke

again. "I rattled off a few things in a row there. Any other favorite things you wanted to mention?"

Cash smiled. "Nah, nothing important. You're good. The whole point was to distract you. That seems to have worked."

"Come on, you're saying your list of favorites doesn't get longer than ice cream and the color blue?" Emmett teased.

"And s'mores. I agreed with you affirmatively on that."

"Anything else?" Emmett asked, prodding.

"Books," Cash said.

"Genre?"

"All kinds. I'm not picky. I just love to read. If I had to pick, I'd probably say biographies. But really I just love the feel of a book in my hands, the sound of the pages turning, the way they smell. If I could get a candle that smelled like old books, I'd be very happy."

Emmett nodded, then said, "Fall, all the leaves changing colors."

"Christmas," Cash replied softly. "The lights, and the music, and the snow."

"Coffee," Emmett said with a grin.

Cash chuckled. "Coffee," he repeated.

"Music."

"You've mentioned it being an outlet before. What do you listen to?"

"I like some of the oldies, like the Beatles and Tina Turner, but I like Adele and Imagine Dragons, OneRepublic, and even Michael Bublé and Josh Groban if I'm in the mood." He flushed slightly and Cash grinned. "They just all have something different to say, you know, and a different way of saying it. They got me through some tough times."

"You won't get any arguments from me," Cash replied. "Michael Bublé and Josh Groban have some awesome Christmas music."

Emmett smiled and it lit up his entire face.

"Do you ever listen to jazz?"

Emmett shook his head.

"You should try it. It can be incredibly relaxing. Just the music, though, without the lyrics. I like to do it while I'm stretching sometimes before bed. Half the time I fall asleep on the floor."

Emmett laughed, and he was smiling contentedly as the flight attendant came by with their snacks and drinks.

"Mmm, this is another one of my favorite things," he said, munching on the bag of tiny pretzels.

"Yeah?" Cash asked.

"Yeah, pretzels, potato chips, anything salty, really."

They finished their snacks shortly and put their tray tables away as the flight attendant came back around for their trash.

"Cupcakes," Cash said, resting his head against the back of his seat, and Emmett smiled. "And donuts."

"Thunderstorms."

"Naps."

Emmett chuckled. "Amen to that." Almost as if on cue, he began to yawn.

"Presents."

"Rainbows," Emmett said. He closed his eyes, once again resting his head against the back of the seat, and Cash smiled. It wasn't long before Emmett was snoring softly, and eventually his head fell to the side and rested gently against Cash's shoulder, his dark blond hair tickling Cash's jaw. He let him stay, breathing in the scent of his tea tree and mint body wash.

And his chest began to ache. Because he knew that he was falling more and more in love with this man, and that this was as close to him as he would ever be.

# Chapter Six

They arrived in DC in the evening and headed straight to their hotel to check in. Emmett and Cash were not the only chaperones but they were the only male ones, and as such they would be sharing a room. They made sure their students were settled and knew the rules: No loud noises, no sneaking out, no drinking, etc. Fortunately, they had a good group of kids and weren't worried about their behavior. They knew if they acted up or misbehaved, they would get hell from their parents, who had paid a bundle to make this trip possible in the first place, and half the students had worked their asses off to pay for the trip themselves.

After making sure the students were settled, they made their way down the hall to their own room, and their eyes widened simultaneously when they opened the door.

"Oh, hell no," they said together, and then looked at each other.

"We did say two beds, right?" Cash said, swallowing.

"Yeah, definitely," Emmett said, his face flushing bright red. "I'll, uh, I'll go talk to them. You can wait here if you want."

Cash nodded and figured he might as well step inside

and sit down. He was exhausted, but not exhausted enough that he was going to crawl into a queen-sized bed with Emmett tonight. Fuck, that would be dangerous territory. Not that he wouldn't secretly love it, but that was the problem. Working with the man every single day was hard enough, and he was only doing that until Mrs. White was back at the school, resuming her position. Sharing a bed with Emmett was so not happening.

But the look on Emmett's face when he returned to the room told him otherwise. His face flushed as he rubbed the back of his neck with his hand and bit the inside of his cheek.

"What is it?" Cash asked when Emmett didn't look at him right away.

"So, apparently the hotel is booked solid, and while they are 'very sorry', they can't do anything about it," Emmett said, walking into the room slowly and shoving his hands into his pockets. "We're kinda stuck here, Cash."

"Oh boy," Cash said, his heart starting to beat a little...okay, a lot faster. He ran his fingers through his hair and Emmett did the same.

Then at the same time they turned to each other and said, "I could sleep on the floor."

"No, you don't have to do that," they both followed.

Now they were laughing a little.

"If anyone's sleeping on the floor, it should be me," Cash insisted. "I'm younger."

Emmett raised an eyebrow at him. "Hey, don't throw that in my face. I'm plenty spry."

Cash flushed. "I just meant..."

"Uh-huh, yeah," Emmett teased. "I'm thirty-one, Cash, not seventy. I can sleep on a floor for a few nights."

"We could take turns," Cash suggested.

"Nah, it's okay. You kept me sane on that plane flight. You should have the bed. Really."

Cash sighed. "Okay," he said reluctantly. He felt guilty but he knew how stubborn Emmett could be and this argument was getting ridiculous.

————

They took turns in the bathroom, brushing their teeth and changing, and Emmett noticed Cash grinning at him when he made his way out of the bathroom.

"Nice," he said, and Emmett followed the other man's gaze to his cheeseburger pajama pants.

"Thank you," Emmett said. "This is another one of my favorite things."

"Ah, I see." Cash grinned. "So, your favorite day would consist of camping, cheeseburgers, s'mores, and stargazing, then?"

*And you.* Oh God, no, he hadn't just thought that, had he? Shit. No matter how hard he fought it, it seemed Cash still had a hold on him. This magnetic young man was intoxicating, and Emmett was starting to panic now, realizing that as much as he didn't want to admit it, he was falling in love with Cash all over again, or maybe, maybe he'd never fallen out of love with him in the first place. Even after five years apart, he'd never actually forgotten about him—the boy with the messy dark hair, the emerald eyes, and the contagious laughter. The boy he'd wanted to dance with, hold close, and kiss soundly on his prom night. Who he'd thought about long after he'd walked away on his graduation day and gone to chase his dreams at Stanford. The boy who was sitting right in front of him now and who was making him seriously think twice about his upcoming wedding.

Oh God. His wedding. He was getting married. In three weeks. To Harper. He was so convinced that he loved her. At least he had been, but now, now he wasn't so sure. And what the hell was he supposed to do about that? He couldn't hurt her. He just couldn't. And he still had no idea if he and Cash could ever work. He didn't know if Cash had any feelings for him at all. God, this was insane.

"Emmett?" Cash said. "You okay?"

Emmett realized he'd been so lost in thought he'd never responded. "Yeah, of course," he lied. "Great. Yeah, that sounds like the perfect day, for sure." He smiled at Cash as the other man went to change.

While Cash was in the bathroom, Emmett grabbed a pillow off the bed along with a blanket from the closet and made his makeshift bed on the floor. He was fairly certain sleeping on the sidewalk would be more comfortable, but he wasn't going to complain.

"You sure you're going to be comfortable down there?" Cash asked when he came out.

"I'm fine, Cash," Emmett insisted, lying on his side, his hands tucked under the pillow. "Go to sleep, okay?"

Cash sighed again and climbed into the bed, turning the lamp off and lying down. "You want another blanket?" he asked. "Or I could turn up the heat. You'll probably get cold down there."

"I'm fine, Cash," Emmett said firmly, but with a hint of a smile to his voice as well. "Good night."

It was several minutes later when he heard Cash's deep voice breaking the silence. "Emmett? You awake?"

"Yeah."

"Is there any reason why we can't share the bed?" Cash said. "I mean, this is kind of stupid. It's plenty big for both of us, and I'm not gonna sleep 'cause I feel guilty that you are on the floor freezing your ass off, and you aren't gonna sleep 'cause you're on the floor, and we have a long day tomorrow, and we had a pretty exhausting day today, so I'm just saying this whole thing is pretty dumb. We're not gonna catch cooties or anything. We can be grown-up about this, right?"

Emmett sighed. He knew in his mind and his heart that he had the best reason ever for not sharing a bed with Cash, but once again he couldn't tell the other man that. *If I share a bed with you, I'm afraid I'll never be satisfied waking up next to Harper again, Cash. That's why.* But truth be told, he was acutely uncomfortable. His thirty-one-year-old body was not handling this whole floor situation as well as he'd bragged that it would. He was already feeling sore. He was damn exhausted from the day of traveling and navigating thirty students through DC, and the thought of doing it again in eight hours after having spent the night on the hotel room floor was less than appealing.

"Emmett?" Cash said when he didn't respond.

"Well, you gonna scoot over or what?" Emmett asked, padding over to the bed, pillow in hand.

Cash smiled a little and shuffled over, and the mattress dipped as Emmett climbed in next to him.

"Goodnight, Cash," Emmett said softly. "Thank you. I'm not as spry as I thought."

Cash chuckled. "Goodnight, Emmett."

———

When Emmett woke up the next morning to the alarm on his phone going off, he was surprised to find that Cash was already out of the bed and in the shower. He rubbed his eyes and yawned, sitting up, then waved his hand in front of his face when he realized just how bad his morning breath was. *Oh God, I hope Cash didn't get a whiff of that.*

A moment later he heard his phone buzzing and saw that it was a text from Harper. He knew something was wrong when, instead of excitement, he felt guilt and fear, but he didn't have time to deal with either of those emotions right now, so he buried them and opened the message.

**Hey, baby, how are you? Didn't hear from you last night. You make the flight okay? Missing you already.**

*Shit.* As if Emmett wasn't feeling guilty enough already, now he'd forgotten to even let his fiancée know he'd made it to DC safely, and she knew how much he hated to fly.

**Sorry, babe, long day. The flight was okay. I have a coworker who helped distract me and make it bearable. Miss you too.**

Her reply came quickly.

**This coworker sounds pretty great. I'll have to meet them some day. You didn't snore like a buzz saw and keep them up all night did you? :)**

Emmett winced. *Crap.* Had he? He knew he snored, more so when he was especially tired, but Harper just shoved him. Then he would wake up, roll over, and go back to sleep, usually pretty quickly. But poor Cash wouldn't have known to do that and it would have kept him up all night. If he'd thought of it beforehand, he would have told him to wake him up. *Damn it.*

Before he could answer Harper's text, the bathroom door opened and Cash walked out. Emmett's jaw dropped at the sight of his former student in a long-sleeve black button-down shirt and underwear. The shirt was covering his rear end, thankfully, but not so thankfully exposing his incredible thighs. Emmett felt his neck heating up and his brain short-circuiting at the sight.

Damn, those thighs were perfection. Not that that was

surprising, given what the rest of Cash's body looked like, but Emmett hadn't expected to get the full picture.

"Sorry," Cash said, catching a glimpse of Emmett, who flushed and looked away. "I had pants in there but they got wet, so I have to find new ones."

"No, it's, uh, it's fine," Emmett stammered.

They had to get out of there, see the city and spend the day with thirty other people, or Emmett was going to lose it and do something really, really stupid.

He hadn't realized just how exhausted Cash looked until he finally had the courage to look him in the face. The man's eyes were bloodshot and his shoulders were slumped. He looked barely conscious. Emmett winced again.

"Did I snore last night?" he asked, grimacing.

Cash glanced at him as he slid on his jeans and fastened his belt. "A little," he said with a shrug.

Emmett eyed him. "Be honest," he said.

"Okay, a metra-fucking ton," Cash said with a smirk. "I wasn't gonna mention it."

Emmett winced. "Sorry. I know it can be loud. Harper's told me. If it happens again, just shove me until I wake up and I'll stop. That's what she does."

Cash nodded. "Okay."

"I'll take a shower now," Emmett said. "Then we should get some breakfast. You look like you could use a few dozen cups of coffee."

Cash chuckled and Emmett disappeared into the bathroom, closing the door behind him. He came out fifteen minutes later dressed in dark wash jeans, a black Henley, and a red leather jacket.

"Wow," Cash said breathlessly, causing Emmett's head to snap up, and he caught the young teacher staring at him, his cheeks flushing a bright red. He smiled at Cash and looked down at his outfit.

54

"Do I look okay?" he asked. Cash cleared his throat and swallowed.

"Yeah," he replied, his voice a touch higher than normal. He tried again. "Yeah, you look good. I mean, comfortable. I mean, I'm not used to seeing you in anything but work clothes." He let out a breath and rubbed his hand across the back of his neck. "Maybe we should go eat breakfast," he suggested.

"Good idea," Emmett said with a smile. They slid their shoes on, grabbed their coats, scarves, gloves, and the key to their room, and headed down to the lobby.

They sat at a table with the other teachers and went over their itinerary while they ate and then made sure all the students were there before heading out for their day in the city.

They visited the White House, Ford's Theater—which was Emmett's favorite as he was a big fan of Abraham Lincoln, the Museum of Natural History, and the Library of Congress, which was Cash's favorite, because of course, books. Emmett practically had to grab him and pull him away when it came time to leave, but he had the biggest smile on his face when he did, because damn if Cash wasn't adorable when he was geeking out over books and history, his green eyes wide, mouth gaping, taking everything in.

"I take it a library, donuts, and coffee would be your perfect day?" Emmett said, coming up behind Cash as he looked around.

Cash turned and grinned at him. "Sounds pretty spot-on."

"You've seen this before, haven't you?" Emmett said, sticking his hands in his pockets and stepping a little closer.

"Yeah, but it's been a long time," Cash replied, awe in his voice as he turned back to the shelves of books. "And I don't think it will ever get old."

Damn if Emmett didn't want to just slide his arms around Cash's waist right then and there and press his lips to the other man's neck, drink in the scent of his body wash and feel his knitted blue scarf tickling his face.

*Engaged. You're engaged. Very, very engaged.*

———

Later that night they took the students to the ice rink at the National Gallery of Art's Sculpture Garden. It was considered a classic winter experience of Washington, DC, and was stunning, particularly at night. The rink was small compared to some of the others in the area, giving it a cozy vibe. Surrounding it was a single string of lights attached to lampposts that illuminated the ice, and behind the posts there were groupings of trees. Couples and families glided about on their skates, smiling, laughing, and occasionally falling. Some of the students and chaperones skated while others sat and talked.

"Let me guess," Cash said, gliding up on his skates and plopping down next to Emmett, where he sat nursing a cup of hot chocolate on a bench, "too close to running to be enjoyable for you?" He grinned, then threw his head back and laughed when Emmett smirked and gave him the finger.

Emmett smiled widely at the sound. He didn't think he'd heard Cash laugh like that since they'd started teaching together. It was the most beautiful sound in the world. He'd almost forgotten how much he loved hearing that deep, carefree, robust laugh.

"You should come join us," Cash said, smiling now. His hair was a tousled mess, his cheeks a rosy pink, his breathing a little heavier than normal from exerting himself, and his smile breathtaking, but Emmett shook his head.

"Sorry, I'm gonna have to pass," he said.

"How come?" He didn't miss the look of disappointment that fell across Cash's face.

"Honestly, it kind of scares me," Emmett admitted. He shrugged.

"Oh, well, in that case, why don't I get us both another hot chocolate, and I'll stay here with you."

"Oh no, you don't need to do that," Emmett said in protest as Cash stood.

"I want to," Cash said. "I'll be right back."

Emmett groaned once Cash was out of earshot but he couldn't deny his desire to spend more time with the younger man.

Cash returned shortly and handed Emmett his drink, which he accepted gratefully.

"You really don't have to stay and keep me company. You should enjoy yourself," Emmett said.

"I am," Cash replied, looking into his eyes, and Emmett felt himself blushing. He cleared his throat quickly and turned to face the other skaters on the ice.

"Did you grow up going skating?"

"Yeah, I guess. We did it every winter. My grandparents owned a house on the lake and we'd visit them for the holidays and my cousins and I would go skating together. We always had really big family celebrations for Thanksgiving and Christmas. What about you?"

Emmett shook his head. "No, it was just us. My parents and my sister and me. We actually moved around a lot when I was growing up. Well, what I consider to be a lot anyway."

"Was that hard for you?" Cash asked sincerely.

Emmett turned to look at him. "Yeah, it was," he said. "It was only three times, but I got pretty attached to places and it was pretty rough on me each time. The first move wasn't a problem. We moved from Colorado to Minnesota. I was only four and I hadn't started school yet or really made any friends. It was just my sister and me. We're only a year and half apart, so we grew up close. The second move was from Minnesota to Wisconsin. I was eight and that was harder because I had made friends. But the third move was the hardest. That's when we came to Indiana. I was starting my junior year of high school and had a boyfriend at the time, and I really didn't want to leave him behind. Or my other friends. I'd assumed I'd be finishing high school where I was, graduating with everyone I'd known for the last few years. I'm a creature of habit and I'm not big on change. I'm getting better with it now, but back then it was..." He trailed off, letting out a deep breath and running his gloved fingers through his hair. "It was horrible."

"Man, that sucks," Cash replied. "That's a rough time for any kid to have to switch schools and make new friends. Why'd you have to move? Was it work related?"

"That's what my parents said, but I'm pretty convinced it was actually because of the boyfriend. Like they thought crossing state lines would fix my sexuality."

Cash frowned. "They don't support you?" he asked.

"My mom does. She's supported me from the beginning, asked me about my relationships, encouraged me to invite whoever I was dating over, whether it was a boy or a girl, but my dad had a harder time with it, and eventually it started causing problems."

"What kind of problems?"

Emmett stared down at his hot chocolate. "They started fighting a lot. I'd hear them in their bedroom, my dad telling her not to encourage me and her telling him he needed to be more supportive. He said some pretty horrible stuff, but she'd always defend me. But it was after that that we moved. I noticed once I started dating a girl my senior year he got happier and started spending more time with me, asked me more questions, but then when we broke up, he distanced himself from me again. It was like he wasn't sure he could be around me if I didn't have a woman on my arm to prove that I was the man he thought I should be. Sure enough, my freshman year of college I started dating a guy again and he flew off the rails. My parents started arguing a lot more; he started getting drunk and violent. He even asked me, if I was attracted to both guys and girls, why I couldn't just choose a girl because it made more sense and it was normal. And didn't I want to be normal? I told him it didn't work like that. That I wanted to be with who I was interested in. Who made me happy. It didn't go well, and he told my mom that she had to choose between me and him because he wasn't going to live with a fag for a son."

Cash swallowed hard. "Shit," he whispered. "And?"

Emmett gave a soft, pained smile. "She chose me."

"Well, good for her," Cash stated. "She made the right choice."

"Yeah, so, anyway, I haven't talked to my dad since then. My extended family is all back in Colorado so we don't see them much. Now I spend the holidays with Harper and we visit her parents for part of it and my mom for part of it, and my sister flies in with her boyfriend when she can." There was a brief pause before Cash spoke.

"I'm sorry about your dad. That must be hard."

Emmett shrugged. "It is what it is. I can't change him, and I can't change myself."

Cash nodded and Emmett flashed a smile at him. "Still, there were some good things about my childhood. It's hard to remember them sometimes with all the shit that happened later on, but we did have some really amazing Christmases and family vacations. My parents were really good about making the holidays special even though it was just the four of us, and honestly I liked it that way. Crowds and large gatherings have never been my thing. It always felt more intimate to me and special to have just us.

"My sister and I would stay up all night Christmas Eve playing board games and watching movies in the basement, and then we'd wake our parents up before dawn. My mom would make cinnamon rolls. We'd have one present out in front of the tree that was the biggest thing or the thing we wanted the most and everything else would be wrapped. There would be Christmas music playing in the background while we took turns opening our presents. Stockings were always first. And we always got a toothbrush and candy, which I thought was apt. I remember the smell of coffee and the cinnamon rolls permeating the house, the lights on the tree that had mismatched ornaments on it. My dad would always have a mug in his hands, complaining about how we woke him up so early, but there would always be a smile on his face." A soft smile crossed Emmett's face and then he found himself blushing. "Sorry, I'm talking too much," he said, sitting up and leaning back, taking another sip of his hot chocolate.

"No, you're not," Cash said fervently. He shook his head. "I like it. That sounds peaceful and wonderful. Tell me more."

Emmett smiled. "My parents would take us on road trips over the summer and we'd just drive, stopping whenever and wherever we wanted to. Then pitch our tents and build a fire, go fishing, have those s'mores." He grinned and Cash smiled. "We'd spend one or two nights some places and entire weeks other places, lose track of what day of the week it was half the time. Go hiking, swimming. My sister and I would stay in the water for hours. My mom tried to scare us out by telling us we'd get all wrinkled and pruny like our grandparents but it never worked." He laughed at the memory.

"I love that," Cash said. "I wish my family had gone on more trips like that, honestly. Our vacations were fun, but I would have enjoyed a little bit more nature."

Emmett couldn't help picturing himself on a camping trip with Cash, sitting around a fire, talking and laughing, eating s'mores and roasting hot dogs, then snuggling under a blanket and...fuck, no, no, no. Shit. Goddamn it. He took a deep breath.

"Hey, what do you say I get some skates and you teach me how it's done out there?" he said, swallowing the last of his hot chocolate and nodding toward the rink.

Cash's eyes widened. "Are you sure? It's really okay if you don't want to. I don't want you to be scared."

"Maybe I won't be as scared if I'm with you," Emmett said. He stood and gave Cash a warm smile. "Come on, let's see how you do teaching something that isn't history."

Cash grinned and followed him.

———

"Okay," Emmett said, leaning on Cash's shoulder as they trudged into the hotel room an hour later. "You are officially the worst teacher ever."

"No, you are the worst student ever," Cash replied, pulling him over to the bed and helping him lie down. "It wasn't me who refused to listen to instructions. You were scaring people to death out there. I think you caused some long-term trauma to those people you bowled over. Especially that little girl."

Emmett grimaced. "I did feel bad about that. She cheered right up after I got her ice cream, though."

"All the ice cream in the world isn't going to keep her

**61**

from therapy. And did you see the way her parents kept her on the other side of the rink after that?"

Emmett chuckled but then groaned. "Every bone in my body aches."

"Yes, well, that's no surprise with the number of times you fell on your ass."

"As the teacher it was your job to keep that from happening," Emmett snarked back.

"It wouldn't have been a problem if you'd gone at the pace I instructed instead of plowing ahead like a bat out of hell," Cash retorted good-humoredly. "That certainly wasn't expected for someone who claimed to be scared."

Emmett shrugged. "I was wrong. It was boring going so slow."

"And safe," Cash said with a smirk and a shake of his head.

Emmett groaned again, gripping his backside.

"What did we learn today?" Cash said, crossing his arms over his chest and staring down at him.

Emmett grinned despite his pain as he looked up at Cash. "That if I'm going to fall, I should at least take you down with me so we both look like idiots and it's a cushioned landing."

"And maybe carry plenty of cash so you can buy off your victims," Cash said, and Emmett laughed.

———

Cash's eyes flew open. His body on instant alert. He had no idea what time it was, only that it was still dark outside and that something had awoken him. Then he realized that Emmett was no longer in the bed next to him, and as he listened he could hear the sound of choked sobs coming from the bathroom. Fuck. What the hell did he do? Leave him alone? Ask what was wrong and try to help? What if he was hurt? Had the ice skating really been that bad? He'd seemed fine when they had gone to bed. He didn't want to embarrass the man, but...fuck that, he wasn't going to take the chance that something was really wrong, either.

He flung the blankets aside and climbed out of bed. Making his way over to the bathroom, he could see the light peeking out from underneath the door. The sounds of Emmett's sobs grew more distinct as he drew closer. Hesitantly, he reached up and knocked on the door. He heard Emmett's breath hitch, then a bang and the other man cursing. He winced.

"Emmett?" he said. "Is everything okay?"

"I'm fine, Cash," Emmett replied, his voice shaky. "Go back to bed."

"You don't sound fine," Cash replied gently. "You're kind of scaring me. Can I come in?"

Emmett didn't respond, so Cash opened the door slowly and peeked inside. Emmett sat on the floor with his back to the bathtub, his knees curled up in front of him and one hand cradling his elbow. That explained the banging sound and the cursing. His eyes were red, his cheeks streaked with tears. His dark blond hair was soaked with sweat, his freckles more prominent than ever under all the perspiration, and his breaths were coming in short gasps as Cash approached and sat next to him on the cold tile floor.

Without even thinking, Cash reached an arm around him and began to stroke his hair, and Emmett leaned into his touch.

"Shit," Emmett said, wiping his tears.

"Shh," Cash soothed. "Just breathe. It's okay. You're okay. You're safe. I promise."

Emmett's head fell onto Cash's shoulder and he shook as he sobbed, but his breathing evened out.

"Is it okay if I'm here?" Cash asked. "I don't mean to make you uncomfortable. I just want to help."

Emmett sniffled and wiped his hand on his pajama pants. "I'm sorry," he said. "I didn't mean to wake you."

"What happened?"

Emmett shook his head. "Nothing."

"Doesn't look like nothing." His gaze flitted over the small bathroom. "You always hang out in the bathroom in the middle of the night? I mean, I get it—it's super cozy, and the company is great..." That earned him a small chuckle from Emmett. "We're friends, right?" He continued to stroke his fingers through Emmett's hair. "So talk to me. What's going on?"

"Nightmare," Emmett said softly. "I get them sometimes."

"Must have been pretty intense."

Emmett nodded and wiped away more tears.

"What was it about?"

"My dad," Emmett said, and Cash flinched. He'd been the one to bring up that subject earlier in the evening. He'd had no idea it would be a trigger for Emmett. "Sometimes I have dreams that we've made up. That he's apologized and accepted me for who I am. That he tells me he loves me, and then I wake up and realize that's all it was. A dream. And it will never be real. More often than not, though, it's a nightmare, reliving the past, the horrible things he shouted at me about what a disappointment I was as a son, how disgusting I was, how perverted. How sick I made him. Why did I have to embarrass him? Why couldn't I be normal? And I feel so much guilt for tearing my family apart and ruining my parents' marriage. Maybe they could have been happy if it wasn't for me, you know? Maybe they'd still be together if I could have just been different, been normal. Or kept my sexuality to myself, stayed hidden."

Cash clenched his teeth, nudging Emmett so that he lifted his head. "Don't say that," he said. "Please. You didn't do anything wrong by being you, and you were the reason I had the courage to be myself. You are one of the bravest people I know. And hearing your story, knowing what I know now, I'm even more convinced of that. You inspire me, Emmett. You always have. I'm sorry you didn't have the support and care you deserved from the people who should have loved you the most. But that's not on you. Like you said to me before, that's on them. And your mom knew that, and she made the right choice. She knew what a gift she'd been given in you. And she's not the only one, right? Or you wouldn't be getting married."

There was a pause, and Emmett swallowed, then shifted away slightly so that their bodies were no longer touching. Cash couldn't help missing the warmth of Emmett being so close to him, and the feel of his body pressed against his. It was a little thing, not romantic at all but intimate nonetheless, and it left him craving more.

"Right," Emmett said. He wiped away more tears.

"Can I tell you something?" Cash asked. Emmett nodded and looked at him, holding his gaze. "I know I told you that I came out to my parents my freshman year of college, but I didn't tell you what led to it." Emmett shook his head.

"I thought a lot about what you said on my prom night after graduation, but as much as I wanted to come out, especially to my parents, the thought was so overwhelming to me. I just couldn't bear the idea of them hating me or being disappointed. And the more I thought about it the more scared I got, and the more angry I got. The more I started to resent the fact that I was gay. I really just wanted to be normal, too. Things started getting really dark. I started drinking, doing drugs, hanging out with the wrong crowd, partying a lot and not focusing on my schoolwork. It went on for months and eventually my grades started declining pretty steadily and I was in danger of losing my scholarship. Of course, my parents saw that but they didn't see the reason behind it. They tried talking to me, asking if anything was wrong, but of course I denied it. I was so scared shitless.

"Then one night I was at a party and drunk and decided I wanted to go back to my dorm, which was across town but didn't have a ride, so I was gonna drive myself." Cash could see Emmett's eyes widening as he continued. "I got hold of my roommate's keys and stole his car, ended up crashing it into a lamppost about three blocks down the road. Thankfully no one but me was hurt, but the car was banged up and I was in the hospital with a concussion and a broken nose and ankle. It was when my parents were visiting me there that I finally broke down and told them I was gay. I just couldn't do it anymore. The grief and anger and everything I was putting myself through was too much and I knew that if I continued on the path I was on, I was going to lose everything. I wanted so much more from life and I wasn't going to get it by behaving the way I was, but I couldn't keep lying to myself and to the people I was closest to. I couldn't keep pretending. And my parents were so scared. That's when they broke down sobbing and told me how much they loved me." Cash had tears in his eyes now as he looked at Emmett. "So please," he said, "please don't say you should have stayed hidden or kept your sexuality a secret, because I know that it would have destroyed you, and you wouldn't be the incredible man and amazing teacher you are now. And you wouldn't have told me the things I needed to hear that saved my life. It was listening to those words and running them through my head over and over again that finally gave me the courage to act."

Emmett swallowed hard and more tears slid down his cheeks. Cash reached out and gently, very gently, cupped Emmett's face in his hands. He heard the other man gasp and felt him jerk slightly but he didn't pull away. In fact his hand came up and rested on Cash's forearm, his eyes locking with Cash's.

"Cash," Emmett breathed, his chest heaving.

Cash brushed his thumbs ever so softly over the tears on Emmett's cheeks, wiping them away, and Emmett's breath caught in his throat. Cash found himself scooting closer, his heart rate picking up as Emmett's gaze lowered, lingering on his lips. Emmett's breath picked up, and he began to lean in too.

"Cash," Emmett whispered again, his breath ghosting over Cash's face, making him shiver. They were so close. Cash wanted him so badly. Wanted to touch, and feel, and explore. Wanted to know what Emmett Jones tasted like, to press his lips to every single one of his luscious freckles and feel the other man come apart underneath him.

He gripped the other man tighter and pulled him closer. "Emmett," he almost growled.

But instead of kissing him, Emmett dropped his forehead to Cash's and gripped his arm, his eyes closed. He was breathing heavily, and he was trembling. "I'm sorry," he whispered, a note of longing in his voice. He pulled away and ever so reluctantly, Cash released his grip. He stared into those beautiful sapphire eyes, his chest aching.

"Thank you," Emmett said eventually, glancing away. "For telling me. I'm, um, I'm really glad you're okay. That was a pretty reckless thing to do. I'm having a really hard time not giving you a lecture. Even though it was five years ago."

Cash gave him a rueful smile as he tried to calm his racing heart. "Believe me, I know. My parents let me have it after they were done telling me they loved me. And I had a good amount of community service to do, too. I'm just glad it wasn't worse. I got really lucky." They sat for a moment before Cash stood and offered his hand for Emmett to take. He pulled the other man to his feet and they made their way back to the bed, climbing in together.

"Goodnight, Cash," Emmett said softly as they faced away from each other.

"Goodnight, Emmett," Cash replied. "Sweet dreams."

When Cash woke up the next morning, it was to find Emmett pressed up against him from behind, his arm wrapped around him, his hand resting on Cash's abdomen. The pressure of his body and the warmth it was giving off made him feel safe and comfortable and whole, made him feel wanted. He didn't move away, just enjoyed the feeling of being in the other man's arms for as long as he could, feeling Emmett's breath against his neck and the sound of his soft snores in the quiet of their hotel room as the light peeked in through the crack in the curtains.

———

"Okay, guys, single file," Emmett said in his most authoritative voice as the rowdy teenagers crowded onto the bus that would take them on their tour of the city the following evening. "Only two people per seat," he added, raising his voice when he saw the students trying to sit on each other's laps.

"That's it, push and shove!" Cash shouted from next to him and gave him a huge smile when Emmett turned and narrowed his eyes. "What? I figure if they do the opposite of whatever you tell them..."

"Oh, that's great," Emmett mocked. "With that philosophy we could stand up in front of the classroom and say, 'Drugs are your friend. The more the better! Drink all the alcohol and forget condoms. Oh, and don't worry about doing your homework. It's for losers.'" He waved his hand in the air carelessly as he spoke and Cash laughed.

The last of the students climbed onto the bus and Emmett followed. There were plenty of empty spots on the lower level of the double decker bus, but even though it would be chillier, the best view was from the top, so that's where he made his way. A moment after he had taken his seat, he heard Cash's voice next to him.

"Mind if I join you?" he asked, giving him that gorgeous smile.

"Of course not," Emmett said, and he couldn't help smiling back.

The stars shone brightly above them as they made their way around to the different memorials under the night sky, the lights of the city illuminating the street and a certain person's deep green eyes.

They'd been encouraged to bring blankets on the tour to keep them warm. Emmett draped the large blanket he'd brought over both Cash and himself. It wasn't long before Cash started to yawn, his eyes closing and his head falling onto Emmett's shoulder as the tour continued. Emmett didn't wake him. He couldn't. He didn't want to. It was his fault Cash had been so exhausted on this trip anyway.

He fought the urge to drape his arm over Cash's shoulders and pull him closer. He was so breathtakingly beautiful, his dark hair sticking up in all directions and tickling Emmett's jaw now, just as Emmett's had done on the airplane a few days before.

Emmett felt tears stinging at the corners of his eyes and wiped them away, fighting doubly hard not to move his face

**69**

ever so slightly and press his lips to Cash's hair. God, he wanted to so badly. He wanted to rest his head on Cash's and close his eyes, wanted to take the other man's hand into his and interlock their fingers together, to cup his stubbled face in his hands and kiss him stupid under the city lights.

Instead, he shut his eyes tightly as more tears fell. Tears of longing and want. Of guilt and regret, shame and hurt. God, he didn't know what he was doing anymore. Nothing in his life made sense.

Tomorrow he would be back on an airplane and heading home to a woman, and a house, and a bed, and a life he wasn't so sure he wanted anymore. Because what he wanted, what he'd wanted for six years, it seemed, was right next to him, as close as it had ever been.

When he woke up the next morning staring into emerald eyes, he found himself wishing he could make this trip last forever because he didn't want to let these moments go.

He didn't want to let Cash go.

# Chapter Seven

Emmett was exhausted when he got back to Anderson. And when Harper slid her arms around his waist at the airport and kissed him, he struggled to kiss him back.

"You okay?" she asked, worry behind her deep brown eyes.

"Just tired," he lied. "I'm sorry." That apology held so many different meanings, ones she had no idea about: sorry for being such a lousy fiancé, for falling in love with someone else when he was engaged to her, for not being who she deserved, for mentally cheating on her, for sucking at life.

God, he was such a screwup. Harper deserved so much better than this, but he couldn't bear the thought of telling her that he was having second thoughts. She would be heartbroken. She would hate him. He already hated himself.

He made up his mind right then and there that this wedding was going to happen. No more second-guessing. No more second thoughts. Harper was a good person, and he cared for her, and she loved him. They were good together. He could be happy with her. He was going to forget about Cash once and for all.

As if to cement the idea in his head, he gripped Harper's arms and pulled her close, pressing his lips to hers firmly, and she smiled.

"Let's go home," Emmett said, smiling back. He took her hand in his as they headed out of the airport.

———

Emmett was more than a little surprised when he was called into Principal Newcomb's office the next day and Cash was there as well. He'd never been "summoned" to the principal's office before. He felt a bit like a delinquent student and wondered what on earth was going on. Was he in trouble? Was he getting fired? Why was Cash here too?

"Good morning, gentlemen," Principal Newcomb said and gestured for them both to sit as he took a seat behind his desk.

Emmett exchanged glances with Cash as they sat, and he could tell from the look on Cash's face that the younger man was just as perplexed as he was.

"Tell me, Mr. Jones, Mr. Christian," the principal started, "how was your trip to DC?"

"Fine, sir," Emmett replied, still confused.

"Any new developments while you were there?" Principal Newcomb folded his hands together and placed them on his desk, looking back and forth between the two men.

Emmett exchanged another glance with Cash.

"Is something wrong, sir?" Cash asked, his anxiety palpable.

"You tell me," Principal Newcomb said. He picked his tablet up off his desk and thrust it toward them.

Emmett leaned forward and took it, his eyes widening.

On the screen was the latest copy of the school newspaper, and front and center was a picture of Cash and him together on the bus trip they'd taken around DC, Cash's head resting on his shoulder, sound asleep, with a caption that read, *Anderson High's Newest and Cutest Couple.*

*Fuck.*

"Care to explain?" Principal Newcomb said, looking between the two of them.

"Uh," Emmett stammered, his heart rate skyrocketing.

"Is there something I should know?" Principal Newcomb asked.

"No," they both said in unison.

"There's nothing in the faculty handbook expressly forbidding staff relationships, but I for one was under the impression that you, Mr. Jones, are very much engaged."

"Yes, sir," Emmett said, his hand trembling as he handed the tablet back to his boss and swallowed. "I very much am."

"Well, there seems to be quite the speculation going around about you two ever since this trip," Principal Newcomb continued. "Apparently, it's not just this picture that's incriminating you. According to your students, you were also sharing a bed, and on at least one occasion, each other's clothes? There was apparently also an instance where you were seen holding hands?"

Emmett's eyes went wide. "Is that all in there?" he asked, gesturing to the tablet.

Principal Newcomb nodded.

"Oh God," Cash breathed. "Sir, I can explain."

"Please do."

"I know it looks bad, especially given Emmett's situation, but I swear it was all just a coincidence. The hotel didn't have any other rooms, so we were forced to share a bed. It wasn't planned. The clothes thing happened because

I spilled on my shirt and didn't have anything else to wear, and Emmett let me borrow one of his, and the holding hands thing was incredibly brief. I stepped into the street without looking and Emmett grabbed my hand to pull me out of someone's way."

"I see. So you are both denying there is anything going on between you two?"

"Yes, sir," they said simultaneously.

"Sir, I'd really rather this not get circulated around the school, and very much not around the town. I'm getting married in two weeks. If my fiancée sees this..."

"Yes, I imagine so," Principal Newcomb said. "This is a draft that the student's sponsor, Mr. Carson, sent to me. He thought it should be looked at and approved before it was published, so it hasn't gone out yet. I wanted to speak to the two of you first. It seems I have some students to talk to."

"Thank you, sir," Emmett said with a relieved sigh.

"You two are free to go," Principal Newcomb said.

Emmett was pretty sure he saw a smile tugging at the man's lips as he stood from his chair and headed for the door, followed closely by Cash.

———

Emmett and Cash both received apologies later that day from the students involved in the newspaper article. The girls were blushing fiercely and looking thoroughly embarrassed when they entered Emmett's room.

"We're so sorry, Mr. Jones," they said. "We didn't mean to complicate things for you. Honestly, we had no idea you were engaged, and to tell you the truth, half the school thought you guys were a couple already anyway, even before the trip. Our bad, though. We're really sorry. I hope we didn't get you into any trouble."

"Thank you, Ava," Emmett said to the short blond, but then stopped her as she headed for the door. "Wait, what do you mean half the school thought we were a couple already?"

Ava looked at the girl next to her and they both blushed. "You know, the way you guys look at each other," she said. "The smiling and the eye sex. We just thought you were already a thing, is all."

Emmett bit his lip and nodded, and the girls turned to leave. He ran his hand over his face and let out a deep breath.

"Emmett?" He looked up to see Cash standing in his doorway.

"Hey," he said.

"Hey." Cash ran his fingers through his hair as he walked into the room. "You just get the formal apology?"

Emmett grinned and felt his cheeks heating. "Yeah."

"Sorry about all that. I can't imagine how stressful that was for you, with your wedding coming up and everything."

"It's okay. It's not your fault."

"I, uh, I actually came to tell you that I'll be leaving soon," Cash said. "Mrs. White had her baby, so she'll be back after the holidays."

"Oh," Emmett said, and he wasn't nearly as relieved as he'd expected to be. "That's, uh...that's good."

"I'm, uh, I'm actually taking a position at a school in California," Cash said, shoving his hands in his pockets.

"Oh," Emmett said again, his gaze leaving Cash's as his heart sank to his stomach. He was finding it difficult to breathe. Cash was leaving for good? He should really be grateful that he wouldn't have to be around him every day, or worry about running into him around town and he could just get back to his life and Harper, but goddamn it, he knew he was going to miss him like crazy.

"Well, uh, good luck, I guess," he said and tried to keep his voice from breaking. Was he really going to cry? Hell no. He wished he could sound more upbeat and supportive for Cash but he just couldn't seem to muster up the false enthusiasm.

"Yeah, thanks," Cash said. He didn't seem any more excited than Emmett felt.

"You ready for a new adventure?" Emmett said, meeting his gaze again. "California. You're going back, huh? That's a long way from home."

"Yeah, I really loved it when I was at Stanford," Cash said. "And I think I could use a new start. Things..." He let out a deep breath. "Things didn't work out here like I'd hoped they would." His eyes met Emmett's and there was a deep sadness in them that mirrored his own.

"What do you mean?" Emmett found himself saying.

"Let's just say I came back to chase some dreams that weren't meant to be, it turns out," Cash said, a sad smile playing at the corner of his mouth.

Emmett's heart clenched. "I'm sorry to hear that."

"Yeah," Cash said. "Me, too." He blinked, his eyes finally leaving Emmett's gaze as he glanced at the floor.

"You're still coming to the wedding, right?" Emmett said, and he found that he could barely get the words out.

Cash nodded. "Of course." His gaze met Emmett's again and he smiled softly. "My flight leaves the morning after, but I wouldn't miss it."

# Chapter Eight

C ash let out a deep breath as he looked in the mirror and cinched his tie, and for what seemed like the millionth time in the last twelve hours, wiped away the tears that slid effortlessly down his cheeks.

He sniffled as he buttoned the sleeves of his suit jacket, wiping more tears away as his chest heaved.

God, he didn't know how he was going to make it through this wedding. How could he sit there and watch Emmett pledge his love and his life to another? Watch them slide rings on each other's fingers symbolizing their life-long commitment, watch him take Harper into his arms and kiss her, dance with her. Watch them smiling and laughing along with all of the other guests who were there to celebrate their love when his heart was aching so badly it felt like it was going to shatter beneath him.

God, it was getting hard to breathe. His hands were shaking as he sat on the bed and slipped his dress shoes on. He swallowed as he stood up, still trembling.

Fuck, he'd known attending this wedding wouldn't be easy, but he hadn't expected it to be this hard. He had to pull himself together. He had to be there. He'd promised

Emmett he would be and he couldn't let him down. After all, this would be the last time he would ever see him. He wanted to see that smile one last time, see those blue eyes lighting up, even if they weren't for him. See that freckle-scattered face, hear that laugh that made his heart melt.

One last time.

He took a deep breath and looked in the mirror once again, wiped away the last of his tears, tucked his tie into his suit jacket, and grabbed his coat.

He had a wedding to go to.

———

Emmett stood in front of the mirror in his dressing room, straightening his red bow tie. He looked at the clock on the wall.

Twenty minutes. Twenty minutes until he would be standing at the altar, waiting for Harper to walk down the aisle.

Twenty minutes until he would have a wife, and then soon after, head to Hawaii on his honeymoon.

This should be the happiest day of his life.

So why was he sick to his stomach? Why did the collar of his shirt feel so tight? Why were his hands shaking when he ran his fingers through his hair? Why did he jump when he heard the knock on the door?

"Come in," he said, his voice sounding weak and shallow.

He expected to see his sister, or his mom, or even the pastor.

"Cash?" His eyes widened when the other man stepped into the room, shutting the door behind him. "What are you doing here? Ceremony's gonna start soon."

He couldn't help noticing how flustered Cash seemed

but also how incredibly handsome he looked in his suit. He also noticed that the man's eyes were red rimmed like he'd been crying, and his face was drawn as if he'd slept very little the night before.

"I know," Cash said, and swallowed hard, his hands clenched into fists by his sides, knocking against his legs. "You, uh...you look very handsome," he said after looking at Emmett for a brief moment.

Emmett blinked. "Thank you," he said, still baffled as to why Cash was visiting him in his dressing room, now fifteen minutes before the start of his wedding. "You came in here just to tell me that?"

Cash shook his head and stepped closer, swallowing once again, face flushed. "No," he said softly, his eyes never leaving Emmett's.

"Cash?" Emmett's heart rate picked up. He stepped back as Cash stepped forward. "What are you doing?"

"Emmett, I...I have to know something," Cash said, stopping inches in front of him.

"What?" Emmett asked, swallowing hard. Cash's eyes never left his face as he spoke.

"Was it just me?"

"What?" Emmett said again, and he was shaking now.

"Was it just me, Emmett?" Cash took a step closer. "These last six years. Was it just me on my prom night that wanted to dance with you?"

Emmett's eyes went wide. His chest started rising and falling. His mouth went dry. What the hell was happening?

"Cash," he said, glancing down, but Cash kept going, stepping even closer.

"Was it just me that wanted to kiss you that night, Emmett?" he asked. "And every night since?"

Emmett looked up, swallowing hard. "Cash, you can't

79

—" he whispered, but the words died on his tongue as tears filled his eyes.

"Was it just me that wished I could take your hand on that airplane to keep you calm?"

Emmett's breath left him. "Cash, please." The tears spilled down his cheeks. "Stop."

Cash was crying now too. "Was it just me, Emmett, that wished that trip to DC never ended so that I could keep waking up next to you every morning?"

Emmett lowered his head again and bit his lip. "Cash, stop," he said again, his chest heaving. A tear fell between them and landed on the floor. "Please. You can't say that."

"I have to," Cash said softly, reaching for Emmett's forearm. "I love you, Emmett."

Emmett looked up at him, eyes wet, cheeks streaked with tears, as Cash's hand moved up to cup his cheek. "What?"

"I love you, Emmett Jones," Cash repeated. "I know you might hate me for saying it, but I had to. I couldn't let you marry Harper without knowing how I feel. I've loved you since my senior year of high school. You were the reason I came back to Anderson. You were the dream I wanted to chase. So tell me, please, was it just me? If it was, then I will walk out of here and get on that plane tomorrow and you will never see me again, I swear."

Emmett just stared at Cash for a moment and then without a word, took Cash's face into his hands and closed the space between them, pressing his lips firmly to his.

God, it felt good to finally kiss Cash, to kiss the boy he'd loved for so long. To feel the other man's lips on his own, his stubble underneath his hands, and to feel Cash eagerly kissing him back.

Before he knew it Cash had him pressed up against the wall. He was moaning as Cash's tongue entered his mouth, carding his fingers through the other man's hair and God, it was glorious. It was everything he'd ever wanted. It was perfection.

But then he was pushing against Cash's chest, and pulling away, shaking his head. "I can't," he said, tears falling once again. "I'm sorry, Cash. I can't."

"Emmett?" Despair clouded Cash's features as his face paled.

"Harper, Cash," Emmett said. "I can't hurt her. Leaving her on our wedding day? What kind of jerk does that? I can't."

"But—"

"I'm sorry, Cash," Emmett said again. He wiped at his tearstained cheeks, tugged his suit jacket down, and readjusted his bow tie. "I've made up my mind. You need to go."

Cash wiped the tears from his cheeks, too, and took in a shuddering breath before heading for the door. "Goodbye, Emmett," he said. "I wish you every happiness."

Then he was gone.

Emmett sat and buried his face in his hands as more tears fell.

# Chapter Nine

Cash wiped at his tears as he sat at the airport waiting to board his plane. He'd left the church after talking with Emmett. He couldn't stick around for the wedding after that. Didn't think he should. He'd just made out with the groom and then been rejected. Surely Emmett would understand. He'd told him to go, after all.

So Cash had gone. He'd booked an earlier flight. He wanted to get as far away from Emmett and Anderson as he possibly could, as fast as he could. He'd put his heart on the line and lost everything, and he couldn't stick around, even for twelve more hours.

California was calling to him. A new job. A new life. A new dream.

He knew it was going to take him a long time to get over Emmett, but he had to start somewhere.

He was sniffling and wiping away more tears when someone sat down right next to him and let out a heavy breath. Cash shuffled uncomfortably, wondering why a perfect stranger would sit so close when there were plenty of empty seats in their vicinity.

Then the stranger spoke, and Cash's breath caught in his throat.

"Hey, Cash."

He blinked and looked up into the striking blue eyes and freckle-scattered face that he loved so very much.

He heard a voice over the intercom just then, calling for his flight to start boarding.

"Emmett?" he said, his eyes blurry with tears. "What are you doing here? Shouldn't you be getting married? Where's Harper?"

"I couldn't marry Harper, Cash," Emmett said, gazing intently into his eyes. "It took me about two minutes after you left to realize I was making the biggest mistake of my life. I went to your apartment to talk to you assuming you would be there, but when I showed up your mom answered the door and said you'd left early. She told me where to find you." He reached over tentatively and took Cash's hand.

Cash felt his chest constricting, but he shook his head as he heard the voice calling for his flight yet again. "Emmett, I have to go," he said, sliding his hand out of the other man's. He picked up his bag and stood.

"No, Cash, please." Emmett grabbed his hand.

"Emmett, you told me to leave," Cash said, tears falling again. "I'm leaving. Please let me go."

Emmett stood, his hand gripping Cash's tighter now. "No. I lost you once to California, Cash, and it took me five years to get you back. I can't let you go." He stepped close enough that there was barely any space between them and gripped the back of Cash's neck, then planted a kiss on his forehead, and Cash closed his eyes, trembling and crying.

"Emmett," he breathed. He brought his hands up to grip the other man's arms.

"I love you, Cash Christian," Emmett said softly, pulling

away. "And it's time for me to take my own advice and chase my dreams. In this case literally, all the way to the airport." He smiled and cupped Cash's face in his hands, looking into his eyes. "You are my dream, Cash," he said. "You've always been my dream. I've wanted you since the first day I saw you in my classroom, sitting in the front row with your wild hair and those breathtaking green eyes. I wanted to dance with you on your prom night more than anything in the world, and kiss you stupid under the stars on that tour bus around DC. I want to wake up next to you every single day for the rest of my life. Please, Cash. Please don't leave."

Cash smiled now as more tears fell, but they were tears of joy this time. Utter and complete joy.

Emmett Jones wanted him. Emmett Jones loved him.

"I can't stay, Emmett," he said.

Emmett's face fell.

Cash chuckled.

"But you could come with me," he said, sliding his arms around Emmett's waist. "Help me look for an apartment. We could spend Christmas break together in California, go to the beach. Go camping." He looked into Emmett's eyes, his own eyes twinkling.

Emmett grinned. "I do already have a ticket," he said. "I had to buy one to get to the damn gate to make my little heartfelt speech to you."

Cash smirked at him. "You're kind of taking all of the romance out of this, Emmett Jones."

Emmett just grinned wider and pressed his lips to Cash's soundly. They heard clapping and cheering around them and pulled away blushing and smiling, pressing their foreheads together.

"So are you coming or what?" Cash asked when they heard the final call for boarding.

Emmett held out his hand and Cash took it.

"I don't have any bags packed or anything," Emmett said.

"We'll figure it out. It'll be an adventure." Cash placed a kiss on Emmett's cheek as they headed toward the plane.

And this time, when Emmett asked Cash to distract him during their flight, it wasn't talking that he had in mind.

# Chapter Ten

"Mmm." Emmett hummed contentedly as he sifted his fingers through Cash's thick, dark hair, enjoying the warm weight of his lover's naked body pressed against his, his cock already standing at attention yet again. He couldn't get enough of this gorgeous man, and the thought that Cash was finally, truly his had his chest constricting as tears filled his eyes. Squeezing Cash tighter to his chest he pressed a kiss to his hair.

Cash had kept him up late the night before. Or rather, they'd kept each other up late. The thought brought a smile to Emmett's face as he stroked his fingers along Cash's bare arm. It had been evening when they'd arrived at their hotel room and Emmett hadn't been sure what to expect. He hadn't wanted to assume anything. He hadn't known how slow Cash wanted to take things. This was all pretty new to them and he hadn't wanted to rush into anything physical. He'd suggested going for a walk or out to dinner when Cash had crossed the room, taken his face in his hands, and kissed him so forcefully it had almost knocked him over.

"I hope you're joking," he'd growled. "Because the only thing I want to do right now is get you naked, Emmett

Jones." And then they were very ungracefully stripping out of their clothes in between hurried, heated kisses, and before Emmett had known it, he was down to his boxer briefs and Cash had him pinned up against the wall once again.

"This is twice in one night you've had me against the wall," he'd teased.

"Shut up," Cash had said, stepping back and sliding off his own underwear, letting them fall to the ground.

"Fuck," Emmett had breathed, once Cash was standing in front of him naked. "God, you're beautiful." There was a small smattering of dark hair over Cash's pecs, and a happy trail starting at his belly button and leading down to the dark thatch of pubic hair surrounding his gorgeous thick cock. It was uncut, bouncing against his flat stomach, already leaking copious amounts of precum. And those thighs, God damn, those thighs. He'd wanted to lick and suck on those thighs until Cash was begging him to let him come. "Come here," Emmett had said, his voice sounding like gravel, and he hadn't missed how Cash's cock twitched at his words. He'd smiled as that firm, slender body moved toward him.

"I'm gonna make you so happy," Emmett had promised as their lips locked again. He'd fisted Cash's cock in his hand and started to stroke him, hearing sounds come out of him that had made his own cock ache for release.

Cash's groans and sighs had filled the room as he'd gripped the sides of Emmett's neck, brushing his nose against his cheek and planting desperate kisses on his freckles as Emmett had stroked him. Emmett's other hand had come around to grip Cash's ass, caressing it and making Cash shiver with the touch. A whimper had escaped the younger man and he'd trembled. "Em." He had swallowed. "Both of us. Do both of us. Please. I want to feel you."

Emmett had smiled. Cash had barely been able to get the words out. He'd used the hand that wasn't wrapped around his lover's cock to free his own erection and then had begun to stroke them in tandem, using their precum as lube. He'd returned his other hand to Cash's silky smooth ass and his eyes had rolled back in his head as he'd heard Cash's moans and whimpers increasing as his climax neared. God, he'd loved the feel of Cash's hard cock in his hand, his lithe, warm body pressed against his, the sounds he'd been making driving him insane.

"Em," Cash had gasped as he'd trembled. "So good. So close."

Emmett had growled. "Me too, baby. You're incredible. Love your cock." He'd removed his hand for a brief second and Cash had whimpered, pressing into him, seeking friction. Emmett had spit in his palm and then taken both of their cocks again, stroking harder and faster, his other hand still kneading Cash's ass cheeks.

Cash had let out a sound that was somewhere between a whine and a moan. He'd buried his face in Emmett's neck, one arm wrapped around his back and the other gripping the back of his head. "Fuck," he'd whined.

"Yes," Emmett had encouraged. "Come for me, Cash. Come on me. I want your spunk all over me."

"Fuck." Cash had gripped onto Emmett's shoulders hard enough to leave bruises, and thrown his head back as his orgasm crashed into him. Emmett's release had followed only seconds later, and he'd let out a low, guttural groan.

"Fuck," he'd breathed, still holding onto both of their cocks as Cash's head came to rest on his shoulder, their bodies slick with sweat, his hand covered in cum that had dripped down his arm and onto the floor. Cash's chest had been rising and falling heavily, and he'd shaken as the aftershocks of his orgasm ran through him. "That was insanely hot. Watching you come...fuck, baby. I've never seen anything like that before. That was gorgeous."

Cash had blushed and smiled, pressing into him and brushing his lips against his neck. He'd still been catching his breath. "I haven't felt that good in a long time," he'd said, and then nuzzled Emmett's neck before kissing it again.

"You better cut that out or we'll being going for round two soon," Emmett had said, his cock already perking up again.

"Is that a threat or a promise?" Cash had looked up at him with a wide smile.

And then Emmett had been gripping Cash's thighs and lifting him as Cash's legs wrapped around his waist, and they'd been kissing fiercely once again.

It had been the perfect night. And he'd woken up with Cash in his arms, his lover's head resting against his chest and his leg flung carelessly over his, pinning him in place, Cash's cock pressed into his hip.

He felt closer to Cash than ever before, and it was incredible. He knew they still had a long way to go, that no relationship was perfect, but he also knew that the love he felt for this man would outweigh any obstacle or struggle that came their way. This was it. Cash was it. He was in it for the long haul.

"I love you," he whispered, pressing another kiss to Cash's hair.

"Love you, too," he heard and smiled at the gruffness in Cash's voice that was so incredibly sexy first thing in the morning. And without a doubt, his cock was rock solid again. How could it not be with this gorgeous, naked man lying on top of him?

"Hmm, you seem to have a situation there," Cash said, pushing himself up on his elbow and grinning at him slyly.

"Shut up," Emmett said. "It's your fault."

"So it is," Cash replied. "I should do something about it, then." He leaned in and kissed Emmett and then slid out of bed.

"Where are you going?" Emmett asked, pushing himself up on his elbows as Cash walked over to his pants, his own dick fully erect now.

"I'm not using spit for what I have in mind," he said, reaching into his wallet and grabbing a condom and a packet of lube. Emmett swallowed.

"You okay?" Cash asked, walking back over to him and sitting on the bed.

"Yeah," Emmett whispered as he began to tear up again. He bit his lip to try and stop the tears from falling.

"What's wrong?" Cash asked, laying a hand on his leg. "We don't have to if you aren't ready. I just thought—"

He stopped talking when Emmett started shaking his head. "No," he said. "No, I'm ready. I'm more than ready." The tears were falling now but he let them come. "God, Cash, I just never thought we'd be here. You and me, making love."

Cash smiled and moved onto his hands and knees so that he was leaning over Emmett, staring into his eyes. "I love you, Emmett Jones," he said, stroking Emmett's cheek. "And I want to be inside you. I want to make you feel so good you are begging for more, and when you come I want it to be with my name on your lips."

Emmett trembled at Cash's words and his cock throbbed with need. The need for Cash to be inside him, for their bodies to be as close as they possibly could be. "Fuck me, Cash," he growled, and pulled the other man down to him, kissing him hungrily.

Cash kissed him back, sliding his tongue inside Emmett's mouth, their moans echoing in the small room. They kissed until their lips were sore and swollen, their cocks pulsing and angry, Cash's precum dripping onto Emmett's stomach and mixing with his own.

"I can't wait," Cash said, his voice rough with need. "I need you, Em. Gonna get you ready, okay?"

Emmett nodded and spread his legs as Cash sat back.

"Fuck, yes," Cash purred. "God, you're beautiful. Gonna fill you up so full, baby."

Emmett groaned at his words, his dick twitching against his stomach. "Hurry up," he begged. "Please. I need you, Cash. I need you so badly." His body felt like it was on fire and ready to explode with the desire he felt for this man to consume every inch of him.

He expected Cash to slick up his fingers to start teasing him open, but instead he lowered his head and gripped Emmett's ass cheeks, spreading them apart. Then he was circling his hole with his tongue, making Emmett gasp and shout his name, gripping the sheets with his hands as Cash's tongue slid over his balls and up his cock in one long stroke.

"Mmm, so good," Cash said, licking Emmett's precum from the tip of his erection and swallowing it down. He gripped Emmett's balls and tugged gently, massaging them, and Emmett bucked. "Shit!" he cried out, drawing in a ragged breath. "Stop torturing me and get the fuck inside me, damn it."

Cash grinned and then he was back at his hole, licking, lapping, and suckling, drawing more and more desperate sounds out of Emmett as he writhed and moaned, bucking his hips and arching his back shamelessly. "Cash! Oh God, Cash," he whined, barely able to catch his breath.

"So beautiful," Cash said breathlessly, lifting his face and wiping the spit from his chin. "God, you make me so hard, Em."

Emmett glanced down just in time to see Cash's face disappear between his legs again and then he was gasping as he felt Cash's tongue delve inside. "Shit!" he cried, his whole body shaking. "Fuck, Cash, I can't." If Cash didn't stop his onslaught, he was going to come and he didn't want that. Not until Cash was buried inside him.

Cash raised his head once again and smiled. He leaned up and kissed Emmett deeply, stroking his cock, which was slick with precum, and Emmett drank him in, savoring the taste of himself on Cash's tongue.

"So hard to stop," Cash said, pulling away. "I love the sounds you make." They both smiled and kissed again. "It won't take long now." He opened the packet of lube and squirted a generous amount onto his fingers. He slid one finger inside Emmett and crooked it just right so that it hit his prostate, and Emmett closed his eyes, moaning as he arched his back, pleasure rushing through him straight to his balls.

"Fuck," he cried. "More, please. I need more." He sounded so desperate but he didn't care. He was desperate —for Cash. Cash added another finger and scissored them, and Emmett whimpered, begging him for his cock. His need for the other man to fill him was so intense he was almost in tears.

"Almost, baby," Cash said. He added a third finger and when he was certain Emmett was ready, he removed his fingers and handed Emmett the condom wrapper. Emmett opened it and expertly slid it onto Cash's thick shaft, then rested back. "I can't wait until we can do this bareback," he said, staring into Cash's emerald eyes. Cash swallowed hard.

"You'd let me do that?"

Emmett nodded, reaching up to stroke his lover's cheek. "I know what I want, Cash, and I don't plan on being with anyone else."

"Me either," Cash said.

Emmett pulled Cash down to him one more time and kissed his lips firmly. "Now fuck me," he growled.

Cash nodded and slicked up his cock with the remaining lube, then positioned himself at Emmett's entrance and slowly began to slide inside. "Oh God, Em, you're so damn tight," he groaned as he bottomed out.

"Fuck, you feel amazing," Emmett said, his chest rising and falling. "I'm not gonna last long, sweetheart."

"Me neither," Cash said, and he started to move, thrusting slowly at first, and then he began to pull out. Emmett practically snarled at him before Cash pushed back in and nailed his prostate once again.

"Oh shit, that's good," Emmett cried, his head falling back against the pillow, his eyes closing. "Right there, sweetheart. Right there. Don't stop. Oh God, Cash, so damn good." He wrapped his legs around his lover and took his face into his hands as Cash continued to thrust into him. Caressing the other man's warm, sweat-slicked skin, he listened to Cash's harsh pants above him, the slapping of skin on skin, and their moans echoing around the room as he gazed into emerald eyes.

"Mine," he growled and kissed him. "All mine."

"Yes," Cash whispered. "Always." He leaned over and kissed Emmett savagely and began to stroke him in tandem with his thrusts. "Come for me, Em," he said. "Say my name, sweetheart. Show me what I do to you."

Emmett cried his lover's name and came hard, ropes of cum shooting out over his stomach and abdomen.

"God, yes," Cash growled, and Emmett spasmed when he felt the warmth of Cash's release through the condom, then smiled as his lover collapsed on top of him.

They lay that way for a few moments, breathing heavily, their aftershocks working through them, before Emmett pressed a kiss to Cash's hair and started stroking his fingers through it. "Love your hair," he said.

Cash lifted his head and kissed him, looking a bit dazed still. "Love you," he said, then slowly pulled out. Emmett whimpered at the loss and Cash smiled as he slid the condom off, tying it and tossing it in the wastebasket next to the bed, before collapsing on his back.

There was a pause before Cash spoke again. He rolled to his side, his head resting on his arm. "Can I ask you something?" He stroked Emmett's side with his finger as he spoke.

Emmett nodded.

"What made you change your mind and come after me?" His gaze locked with Emmett's and Emmett didn't look away. Cash deserved to hear this. He took Cash's hand in his and brought it to his lips, pressing a kiss to his fingers and then holding it against his chest.

"Honestly, it was when you told me that you wished me every happiness that I realized I wasn't happy and I wasn't going to be happy without you, as much as it would hurt Harper. I was making my decision with everyone's feelings in mind but my own. I was so worried about what Harper would think, and about what the rest of our families would think and letting people down, but I never realized how much I was letting myself down or how much it was hurting me, not taking my own feelings into consideration. And I couldn't do that anymore. I thought about what you said, about being true to myself and how if I hadn't done that back in high school and college, it would have destroyed me, and you were right. I didn't want that. My happiness mattered and I realized that. I realized that you were my happy place, Cash. You always have been."

Cash smiled as tears glistened in his eyes. He leaned over and pressed a kiss firmly to Emmett's lips, humming into his mouth as their tongues tangled. "You know you're not bad at this, for an old person," he said, pulling away and smiling, a twinkle in his eyes.

Emmett's mouth fell open but he couldn't help the laughter that escaped him as he chased after Cash to the bathroom, smacking him on the ass when he caught up with him, the other man laughing and squirming in his arms.

After getting cleaned up, Cash let Emmett borrow some clothes and they went out for breakfast before doing some shopping so that Emmett would have a few things of his own. He would only be in California for a couple of weeks but that was long enough that he couldn't be borrowing Cash's clothes the entire time.

"Hey, I got you something," Emmett said as they sat down to lunch later that afternoon. He pulled out a small paper bag and handed it to Cash, who took it with a raised eyebrow, but the look on his face when he opened it was absolutely priceless, and Emmett couldn't stop smiling.

"Em," Cash said, pulling out the candle and lifting it to his nose. He breathed it in and his eyes started to fill with tears. "You got me a candle that smells like old books." He wiped the tears from his eyes as he smiled from ear to ear. "Shit." He laughed and got up from his chair, taking Emmett's face in his hands and kissing him soundly right in front of the entire restaurant. "Thank you," he said, looking into his eyes.

"You're welcome," Emmett said, his eyes dancing with love, laughter, and adoration. "I'm going to spend the rest of my life making you happy, Cash. In every way possible." He squeezed the other man's hand.

"All I need for that to happen is you, Emmett Jones," Cash said, and Emmett was certain that he meant it.

# Epilogue

**Two years later**

"Cash!" Emmett called from the bedroom. "Baby, have you seen my green tie?"

He was almost ready for work but that damn tie was eluding him and his husband wasn't answering, so he gave up and grabbed his red-and-white striped one instead. He was heading to the kitchen tying it around his neck when his face split into a huge grin.

Cash was sitting on the kitchen counter wearing a dress shirt, tie, underwear, and socks but no pants. He held a donut in one hand with a bite missing, a book in the other, and he was laughing.

Emmett couldn't believe how damn adorable he was.

"Morning, gorgeous," he said, walking over to him and placing a kiss on his cheek. Cash smiled at him. "Not that I'm complaining or anything," he added, his eyes sparkling as they took in his husband's naked legs, "but where are your pants, babe?"

Cash chuckled, looking down at himself. "They're in

the dryer," he mumbled through a mouthful of donut. "I'm waiting for them to get done."

Emmett hummed and stepped in between Cash's legs, sliding his arms around his husband's waist and pulling him closer. "I've got an idea for how we can pass the time," he said, his voice low and sultry as Cash leaned in. And then, instead of kissing his husband, Emmett turned his head and took a bite out of his donut.

Cash stared at him, eyes wide, and Emmett laughed heartily.

"You dick," Cash said, but laughed as well. "You better kiss me after that."

Emmett did, and it quickly grew more heated. Cash put his book and donut aside and wrapped his legs around his husband's waist as they ran their fingers through each other's hair, moaning softly.

"Fuck," Cash said, pulling away, Emmett's hands sliding along his bare legs. They were both breathing heavily.

"It's your fault," Emmett teased. "You know what these legs do to me."

Cash grinned. "I also know that you, Mr. Jones-Christian, are nothing if not well versed in the art of self control, and we have to be at work in twenty minutes." He pressed his lips to the tip of his husband's nose and unwrapped his legs from around his waist.

Emmett huffed.

"Later," Cash said, grinning.

"Promise?" Emmett said, a pout on his lips.

"Scouts honor," Cash promised, giving Emmett a salute. "As soon as 4 o'clock rolls around, we'll peel out of the school parking lot together, race home, and you can show me how the old people get down and dirty." He grinned at his husband.

Emmett smirked. "You ever gonna let up on the fact that I'm a mere eight years older than you?" he asked, crossing his arms over his chest.

"Probably not," Cash said. "It's too much fun."

Emmett grinned and kissed his husband, then grabbed a bagel with cream cheese for breakfast. They both brushed their teeth, Cash threw his pants on and tucked in his shirt, and then they grabbed their coffee thermoses and made their way to work.

Living in California was wonderful, and Emmett loved it. Not only was he married to the love of his life, but he was close to his sister now, too. Cash and he had been married for the past year and a half. Cash had proposed to him on a camping trip they'd taken together, and they'd only been engaged for a month before they'd tied the knot. They hadn't seen any point in dragging things out and waiting any longer. They'd known what they wanted. They'd had a small ceremony, just family. Emmett hadn't been ready to go through a big wedding again after the situation with Harper. He had still been dealing with some of the fallout from that. He'd hurt and upset a lot of people, he knew. His family and friends had been supportive, but Harper's not so much. He couldn't blame them, but he'd needed a restart, and so he'd quit his job in Anderson and moved to California with Cash, found a job there at a school not too far from the one Cash was teaching at, and when a position had opened up at the same school that had fit Emmett perfectly, he'd jumped on it.

And now they were free to chase their dreams together.

*The End*

———

Want to read Cash and Emmett's engagement story? You can get it for free, along with other short stories still to come by signing up for my newsletter here: felicitysnow.substack.com

# Acknowledgments

A special thank you to Jen Sharon for her invaluable insight and for helping me make this story the best that it could be. I'm so glad you were on my team. I wouldn't have made it this far without your support and encouragement. And to Jennifer Smith for making my work shine.

Credit to GetCovers for the wonderful cover design.

# About the Author

I'm a mom, wife, and a lover of both reading and writing mm romance. I live in sunny Florida with my family and our fur ball who has been with us since he was a puppy. I love sunshine and rainy days, curling up with a blanket and a good book, or watching my favorite tv shows. I love coffee and hot chocolate and consider Starbucks to be self-care :) I love to shop, craft, sing, and just create in general, which is why writing is such a passion.

You can follow me and visit my website here:

linktr.ee/felsnowauthor